Born in Warwickshire, Heather has spent a major part of her adult life in Australia where she lives with her husband and daughter. She regularly attends the races in Melbourne where the sport is associated with fashion and fun. The yearly Spring Racing Carnival attracts overseas visitors to compete for the famous Melbourne Cup, and this was the inspiration for her previous novel, *Flying Colours*.

RED FOR DANGER

Leaving behind a career in an American soap opera, Foxie Marlowe returns to Melbourne to comfort her recently widowed mother and take over her father's racing stables. However, she learns that during her father's illness, Daniel Morgan — the son of a family friend and the man with whom she once had an affair — rescued the business. Foxie believes that Daniel has taken advantage and stolen her inheritance, until he convinces her to join him as a business partner. Ignoring her lawyer's advice, she invests both her money and emotions in Daniel. But can she really trust him?

Books by Heather Graves
Published by The House of Ulverscroft:

FLYING COLOURS

HEATHER GRAVES

RED FOR DANGER

Complete and Unabridged

ULVERSCROFT
Leicester

First published in Great Britain in 2006 by
Robert Hale Limited
London

First Large Print Edition
published 2007
by arrangement with
Robert Hale Limited
London

British Library CIP Data

Graves, Heather
    Red for danger.—Large print ed.—
    Ulverscroft large print series: romance
    1. Television actors and actresses—Fiction
    2. Horse racing—Australia—Melbourne (Vic.)—Manage-
    ment—Fiction 3. Love stories 4. Large type books
    I. Title
    823.9′2 [F]

    ISBN 978–1–84617–780–4

Published by
F. A. Thorpe (Publishing)
Anstey, Leicestershire

Set by Words & Graphics Ltd.
Anstey, Leicestershire
Printed and bound in Great Britain by
T. J. International Ltd., Padstow, Cornwall

This book is printed on acid-free paper

1

He moved closer, crowding her, forcing her back into a corner of the room until there was nowhere left for her to go. He took hold of her arms and pulled her roughly towards him, making her gasp, his voice hoarse with suppressed emotion. 'Don't do this to me Carole — you can't leave. You have to give me one more chance.'

She glared back at him, shaking her long, red hair down her back. Deliberately, she drew herself up to her full height and stared into the powerful studio lights until they brought real tears to her eyes. 'I don't have to do anything, Raven,' she said at last. 'Not any more. You've betrayed me once too often and this time I'll never forgive you. Never.'

She held the pose long enough for the camera to move in slowly for a final close up, allowing one of the tears to spill over and run down her face.

'And cut.' The assistant director called an end to the scene, allowing the actors to relax. 'Thanks guys, that was great. We're all done for today.'

'I don't think so.' The actor playing Raven

stopped him, grabbing his arm. 'I want another take. Didn't you see what she did? Towering over me, hogging the scene and making me look a fool.'

'Not that you need any help to do that,' the assistant director muttered, half to himself. 'You don't get it yet, do you, pal? You're here to make Jane Marlowe look good and that's all. Jane as Carole Parker — she *is* the show. Nobody gives a damn about you.'

Unwilling to join what looked as if it was developing into a lengthy argument, Jane hurried from the set to catch the executive producer while he was still in his office. It had been a long afternoon already and nobody wanted to hang around once the day's shoot was in the can.

Cameron Carstairs was still there, on the phone as usual but he smiled and waved at her to come in when she knocked and stuck her head round the door. He would always find time for his favourite star. He finished his phone call and leaned back in his chair, smiling at her and steepling his hands. In his late thirties, Cameron was at the pinnacle of his career, producing *The Brave and the Free*. The show had surprised everyone by turning out to be one of the most successful American 'soaps' of all time. And he knew just how much he owed to this leggy

2

Australian girl who had started with him as a fresh-faced teenager and now, ten years down the track, was the mainstay of the show.

'I've been expecting you,' he said. 'Your contract's coming up for renewal, Jane. We should discuss it.'

'Yes Cam, I know,' she said softly, aware that he wouldn't like what she was going to say. 'We need to talk.'

'That sounds ominous.' He caught the inflection in her low-pitched, expressive voice. One of the things he loved most about her was that voice. When he first heard it, it had sent shivers down his spine. It still did, but he was enough of a professional to keep his mind on the job. 'Now don't tell me your agent's putting you up to ask for more money because right now I can't see my way clear to offer a pay rise to anyone — '

'No, Cameron, it's not that.' She was quick to reassure him. 'This isn't about money. My father died and I need to go home — to Australia.'

'But that's terrible, Jane.' He sat back to look at her, his face creased in genuine sympathy. 'I'm so sorry. When did it happen?'

'Last week.'

'Last week? But why didn't you tell me? We could have — '

'No point. We all knew it was going to

happen, if not exactly when. We'd already said our goodbyes. All the same, it's hard to believe that he's gone.'

'I'm sure.' Cameron bit his lips, looking thoughtful. 'Now you take as much time as you need — we'll work around it — write you out for a month or so.' He brightened. 'Carole Parker will take a long trip overseas.'

'Cam, you're not hearing me. I can't sign a new contract. My mother needs me. This time I want to go home to Melbourne for good.'

He stared at her for a moment, not quite believing it. 'Darling, no. *The Brave and the Free* can't possibly go on without you. Carole Parker is our bitch queen, the one everyone talks about, the most loved and hated character in the show. We can't afford to lose her or have her played by anyone else — the fans wouldn't stand for it.'

'We could kill her off. Nothing like the shock exit of a central character to send the ratings sky high.'

'For a while.' He frowned, considering this, less sympathetic now. 'But from where I'm sitting, it looks like killing the goose that lays the golden eggs. I'm not finished with Carole yet. She has a whole lot more left to do.'

'Does she?' Jane's smile was wry. 'Look at her. She's been married four times — twice to the same guy. She has three children who ought to be infants but somehow they've fallen into a time warp and bypassed primary school to turn up as teenagers — '

'Teenagers are more interesting — rebellion and premature sex — all that juvenile angst.'

'But aside from all that, what about Carole herself?' She took a deep breath before going on. 'She's survived car crashes, been dragged out of burning buildings and must have had every form of surgery known to man — except maybe a brain transplant.'

'This is soap country, darlin',' he drawled. 'Don't look for reality here.'

'I know that. But even if I wasn't needed at home, after ten years of Carole, I've had enough. Let me go out on a high, before I get stale. It must be time to see a fresh face on the show?'

'We can have a fresh face or two without losing Carole,' he grumped. 'And anyway, what will you do with yourself in Australia?' He made it sound as if it were the wastes of Antarctica. 'I suppose they do have some sort of local TV?'

'Oh yes,' she teased, trying to lighten his mood. 'We have progressed beyond Dad and Dave on the radio.'

He wasn't to be diverted. 'But it won't be

the same as LA. And what happened to all that drive and ambition? You always wanted to get into mainstream movies?'

'Once maybe I did. But I've stayed so long with *The Brave and the Free* that everyone sees me as Carole now; I'll never be asked to play anyone else.'

'Which all adds up to a first-class reason to stay.' He thought about it a moment. 'So what *are* you going to do? Marry a millionaire? Surely, you can't retire. Not at your age.'

'I'm going to train horses. Racehorses.'

He grinned, about to laugh it off as a joke until he saw she was serious. 'You're not kidding, are you? Hell, Jane, I didn't even know you could ride. We could have used that.'

'I don't. Not all that well, anyway. We have professionals to do that. But horses have been a part of my life for as long as I can remember. I used to work with my father during our long summer breaks. He made me promise to keep it all going after he'd gone.'

'Don't you have brawny Australian brothers to do that?' Cameron was beginning to realize how little he really knew about her.

'Nope. Only me. Our stable manager is a licensed trainer and we have good back-up in grooms and stable hands. But the driving force behind it all will be me.'

6

'Think about it Jane: this is crazy. To turn your back on all you have here for the sake of honouring a promise like that. I suppose there's money in racing but — '

'Cam, I already told you, this isn't about money. It's about loyalty and tradition, keeping a family business alive.'

Cameron frowned. 'I still think you're letting sentiment cloud your judgment. Training a bunch of country nags in Australia, what a waste of your time.'

'That depends on your point of view.' Her temper flared. 'Some people think soap operas are a waste of time.'

'Yes, well . . . ' he bit his lip and winced, aware he had made her angry. He hadn't meant to do that.

'For your information, horses bred in Australia and New Zealand are among the finest in the world. My father worked hard to build a reputable racing stable and I'm not going to let it fall apart. We have loyal workers who are depending on me.'

'Why? Surely, they know it's only a job and can't last forever? They'd leave you fast enough if it suited them. It's not up to you to save the world.'

'No,' she said lightly. 'Just my little corner of it.'

He sighed. 'Jane, I hate to ask you this but

I must. Can't you take a break to set things straight over there and then come back to give us just one more year?'

'And another and another at the end of that? No Cameron, I can't. Mum seems to be holding it together at the moment but I don't think she realizes how much she depended on Dad. She's going to need me when reality sets in. And although I've lived in LA for ten years, it's never been home to me. I have no real ties.'

'And whose fault is that?' he murmured, pulling his bottom lip. Having a solid reputation as a ladies' man with three marriages behind him, Cam had never been able to understand why this particular woman evaded him. 'I suppose you've got some hunk tucked away in Australia?'

'Not really,' she murmured, although his comment brought to mind, however unwillingly, that brief but tempestuous affair with Daniel Morgan. The memory of it still made her blush. Daniel Morgan of all people when she really ought to have known better.

The first time they met she was four years old. He had tried to drown her in her own paddling pool. It was her birthday and their mothers were sitting nearby, expecting their children to play nicely together. Instead, it had been hatred at first sight.

'Don't like girls,' Daniel said, pulling a face and hitting the water to splash her.

'And I don't like boys!' she yelled, splashing him in return and sticking her tongue out for good measure. 'Slugs and snails and puppy dogs' tails. And they smell!'

Having no answer for this, Daniel seized her topknot of red curls and tried to shove her face downwards into the water. Fortunately, her screams alerted their mothers who quickly came to the rescue. All the same, it took several minutes to pull the angry children apart, leaving all four of them soaked and breathless.

'Your son has a filthy temper,' Marion glared at her friend as she tried to comfort her sobbing, red-faced daughter who was still gasping for breath.

'No worse than your daughter's,' Rose was quick to point out. 'Little harpy. Didn't you hear her screaming at him?'

This was the closest the two friends ever came to having a quarrel, reminding both that it was unwise to criticize other people's children. For the sake of peace they decided to keep them apart and Jane was happy as well as relieved to hear that Daniel had been sent away to school.

She didn't see him again until they were both sixteen when he was invited with his mother to attend her own mother's fortieth birthday party. She was surprised to see he had grown into a handsome, athletic boy without a hint of acne or puppy fat; the kind of boy she and her friends only dreamed about. Seeing how well he had turned out, she would have buried the hatchet there and then except he had other ideas. He wasn't impressed by the lanky teenager who slouched in a corner, hunching her shoulders in the hope of drawing attention away from her height.

'Well, well,' he said. 'Jane, isn't it? Fancy seeing you after all these years.' He peered at her and she held her breath, hoping that he might say something nice.

'You've got a zit on your chin,' he said at last. 'Almost ready to burst.'

The resounding slap she gave him could be heard even over the music and conversation, shocking everyone into silence.

Eight years were to pass before they saw each other again. Daniel went away to veterinary college in England, spending most of his holidays with cousins in Ireland and in the meantime she went to LA to be in the show. They didn't meet until she was home on one of her long summer breaks and he brought a horse over from Ireland for her father to train. Although he didn't know her

10

at first, she recognized him immediately and stuck her nose in the air as she swaggered past him in the stables.

'Wow,' he spoke to her father under his breath. 'Grooms are getting good-looking these days. Who's that gorgeous girl?'

'Surely, you recognize Foxie?' her father had answered him, using her family nick-name. 'Big star she is now — in LA.'

Having learnt her lesson with Daniel before, Jane tried to keep out of his way while he was equally determined to pursue the ugly duckling who had turned into such a very desirable swan. And although the relationship got off to a shaky start, Daniel having to spend a lot of time convincing her that he was no longer the crass teenager she had known before, the chemistry between them was impossible to ignore.

Looking back on it now, she could see that a love affair with the son of a family friend could only end in disaster, but it hadn't seemed that way at the time. Daniel Morgan, broad-shouldered, so handsome it was almost unfair and fit from both riding and working out. One of the few men she had ever dated who had sufficient height to allow her to indulge her passion for high heels. Taller than most men, even without them, she had found it exhilarating to lie in bed with someone with legs long enough to entwine with her own. The sex had been wonderful, too. Daniel was nothing if not an exciting, innovative lover and she'd had sense enough not to ask where he gained his expertise.

But when it came to planning a future together, they soon hit the wall. He refused to understand about her career in LA. She was shocked to find he expected her to give it all up and stay home.

'But why, Foxie? Why do you have to go back?' he had said, refusing to see reason and flying off the handle as he always did when he didn't get his own way. 'You're not even making real movies, just pap for the masses. Candy floss for the mind.'

'Don't you dare belittle my work.' She glared back at him, her own temper quick to rise. '*The Brave and the Free* is one of the most successful soaps of all time, watched in over a hundred countries all round the world.'

'Yeah. A testimony to most people's bad taste,' he flung back at her.

'And aside from anything else, I have a contract.'

'Break it,' he said dismissively. 'What can they do?'

'Sue me, for a start, and make sure I never work in that town again. Daniel, please try to understand. I can't leave the show without causing a major upheaval. And to be perfectly honest, I don't want to. Not right now. I can't let everyone down.'

'No. you prefer to let *me* down instead.'

'You're a fine one to talk. You have no loyalty to anyone, hopping from one career to another. You couldn't even stick at being a vet.'

'That's enough, Foxie. You're crossing the line.'

They had parted with many more bitter words, each accusing the other of selfishness. She hadn't heard from him since and was too proud to call him and make the first move. As their mothers remained good friends, she did hear about him from time to time, steeling herself to learn that he was married or at least engaged. So far this hadn't happened although the latest news was that he was involved with some French girl named Suzette. Jane felt more than a stab of jealousy until she reminded herself it was over between them and Daniel was free to do as he liked. All the same, her heart sank at the thought of seeing him with a wife.

'No.' She sighed, hauling herself back to the present and Cameron's raised eyebrows. 'I don't have anyone waiting for me back home.'

★   ★   ★

'Mother? Mother, are you home?' Rose winced as she heard the back door slam in the wake of her son's arrival. He never called her 'Mother' unless he was angry and she had a pretty good idea what was making him angry now. She pushed her needlepoint under a cushion and sat up straight, ready to brave the storm of her son's displeasure. Daniel had a temper to match the dark flame of his hair; devil's hair, his father had called it on the day he was born.

'Will you look at that — bright red hair and a face to go with it,' his father had said, trying to soothe the squalling baby who could wave his fists in fury even at that tender age. 'What a temper.'

She had no further time for such reverie as Daniel confronted her, hands on hips, angry sparks almost shooting from his cat-like golden-brown eyes. Rose looked back at him, thinking that even with his face creased in lines of ill temper, her son was still a devastatingly handsome man. No wonder girls fell for him like ninepins.

'What did you do to Suzie?' he demanded, coming straight to the point.

'Me?' Playing for time, his mother shrugged, feigning innocence. 'Nothing. I didn't do anything.'

'What did you *say* to her, then? To make her give me my marching orders?'

'Has she, dear? Oh, what a shame.'

'Come off it, Mum. You know very well she did.'

Rose considered this comment before she spoke. 'Suzette was a very sweet girl, but a little bit spineless, I thought — '

'Not so spineless she couldn't find the courage to give me up. Hopped on a plane she has and gone back to Europe to join her parents. They're retiring to some broken-down cottage in rural France. Now she'll marry some fat Frenchman with a vineyard who'll give her a baby every year.'

'Yes and be very much happier than she would have been, married to you.'

'What do you mean?' Daniel started to pace the room. 'Every time I get a new girlfriend, you scare them off. An unnatural mother, that's what you are. Most women want to see their sons married and giving them grandchildren.'

'So do I. Nothing would please me more. Soon as you find the right girl.'

'And how many 'wrong' girls' hearts do I have to break before we find someone to suit you?'

'*I'm* not the one who has to be suited — '

'No? You could have fooled me.'

'Daniel, stop it. You don't even realize how you browbeat people. You're doing it right now to me. Your father was just the same — '

'Ah now, don't let's bring *him* into this. Isn't it bad form to speak ill of the dead?'

'Not if it's true. Your father had all the charm in the world, just as you do. But I didn't find out until after we married that he had the temper of Old Nick combined with an obsessive determination to get his own way. It shocked me when I saw it the first time but luckily I could stand up to him. We had a stormy relationship but it was exciting, just the same.' Rose flushed and her eyes lit up for a moment until the memory of his death took the sparkle away and her shoulders slumped. 'But if he hadn't drowned himself learning to water-ski, we might not have gone the distance — and sometimes I wonder about that. Suzie wasn't for you. A gentle soul like that would never have been able to stand up to you.

'Aha! Now I see where this is going. You won't be satisfied till I find someone exactly like you.' He struck a pose, dropping to one knee and starting to sing, 'I wanna girl, just like the girl — '

'Oh Daniel, stop it.' Rose covered her ears and winced at his tuneless singing. 'I told

16

you, *I'm* not the one who has to be satisfied. But I know you'd never be satisfied with a doormat like Suzie.'

He gave a slow handclap. 'You do a good hatchet job, don't you Ma? Poor old Suzie. In the last five minutes she's been *spineless, too gentle a soul* and *a doormat.* The girl did love me, you know.'

'No, she didn't. She loved the *idea* of you, that's all. You should thank your stars. I've saved you from the heartache and pain of a messy divorce. The moment she saw your temper, she'd have been on the next plane for France, anyway. So,' she concluded with a happy smile, 'same result but with only half the expense.'

'How do you do it, Ma? You even manage to make it sound reasonable.' He threw himself into a chair and smiled at her ruefully. 'OK, I'll let it go this time because you're probably right. Suzie could well have been crushed under the weight of two strong Morgan personalities. I'm sure Dad wasn't the only one who liked to get his own way. But from now on, there'll be no more interference or you really will see the sparks fly.'

'Oh sure.' Rose shrugged it off with a mischievous smile. 'But never mind that now. I have much more interesting news.'

'Oh?' Suspicious again, he glanced at her through narrowed eyes. 'And what might that be?'

Rose smiled, hardly able to contain her excitement. 'Foxie Marlowe's coming home — and this time, Marion says, it's for good.'

★   ★   ★

Jane was tired. It had been a long flight and as soon as she left the plane she took the opportunity to visit the rest rooms to redo her make-up and change. Although she had left the show, her character would remain on the screen for a month or so and she owed it to her fans to present them with a well-groomed, sophisticated vision of Carole Parker, not a bedraggled creature suffering from jet lag.

She brushed out her hair and tied it back in a high ponytail, making her streak of premature white hair more prominent than ever. A family characteristic, it arrived in her early teens, an even more striking contrast against a background of curly, red hair. Combined with her high cheekbones and hazel eyes, it had earned her the nickname of Foxie at school although she had taken care not to let it follow her to LA. There she had never been anyone other than Jane.

Using concealer to hide the dark circles that grief and the long plane journey had smudged beneath her eyes, she made up quickly and skilfully, using brushes and eyeliner as well as bronzers and rouge to combat her weariness and bring a sparkle to her eyes. A spray of Silver Rain, her new favourite perfume, lifted her spirits.

Satisfied with her appearance, she tweaked her new apple-green linen suit into place and went to collect her luggage from the carousel before heading through customs.

'Carole Parker!' It wasn't long before a woman let out a shriek behind her. 'There!' she said, jabbing her friend in the ribs. 'I told you it was her.'

Seconds later, she was surrounded by a small crowd of adoring fans, brandishing pens and demanding autographs on arms, airline tickets and anything else that came to hand.

'Ssh!' she said, confiding in them afterwards as she put on dark glasses to hide her eyes. 'I need your help to find a trolley and get out of here quickly before I get stopped by anyone else.'

Her fans were only too willing to push her luggage and provide the cover she needed and she was able to slip through customs without any further event.

After thanking them, she took charge of her trolley and pushed it through the main hall, searching the waiting crowd for a familiar face — one of her cousins perhaps. She knew her mother wouldn't come; she loathed driving through the city at the best of times. At last she saw a large sign held high at the back of the crowd. *Foxie Marlowe* it read. They'd sent a chauffeur, then. Somehow she felt disappointed, a little let down. After travelling so far and looking forward to coming home, she had expected someone to make the effort to come to the airport to welcome her. Nevertheless, she made her way to the sign and announced herself to the tall man in a dark suit standing behind it.

'I'm Foxie Marlowe — '

'Yes ma'am, I know.' The sign came down to reveal a smiling Daniel behind it, making her heart leap as she recognized him. Now she was doubly pleased she had taken the time to freshen up.

In the four years since she had seen him he had filled out and grown into his lanky frame. His shoulders no longer looked too broad for the rest of his body. He looked comfortable with himself as the man he now was, confident of his powers. How was it that men could do this so effortlessly, while women had to work so hard to keep face and figure? No doubt he was aware of the devastating effect that his slow smile and golden brown gaze must have on the opposite sex. But recalling the harsh words that had passed between them the last time she saw him, she was determined not to fall for his charms yet again. Consequently, she spoke more sharply than she intended.

'Daniel Morgan. Well, what a surprise,' she said without offering her cheek to be kissed. 'You're the last person I expected to see.'

'I'm sure,' he said, leaning forward to kiss her anyway and making her widen her eyes. He smelled wonderful, of spicy, masculine good health and the expensive cologne he favoured. She remembered it well from their time together although she had forgotten the name. She felt hot colour rising to her cheeks as memories crowded in on her but if he saw her discomfort, he chose to ignore it, remarking on the large amount of luggage she carried instead.

'Quite a pile you have there,' he said.

'Not really when it's all I have in the world,' she gave a wry smile. 'Everything else was sold off. I'm not going back.'

'So I heard.' Now it was his turn to look less than comfortable. 'And as this is a small town after all and we're bound to run into each other, Mum said it was high time we buried the hatchet and learned to get on.'

'Oh?' she said, still prickly, and hoping he didn't realize how much just the sight of him had unsettled her. 'So this was her idea, was it? Not yours?'

'Not entirely,' he said easily, producing the single red rose he had been hiding behind his back. 'Will this do instead of an olive branch?' Once again he smiled into her eyes, making her heart lurch. 'It's good to see you again, Foxie, I mean it. Welcome home.'

She accepted both his sentiments and the rose, closing her eyes to breathe in its gorgeous perfume as well as to calm her thumping heart. It wasn't the usual antiseptic, hot house rose from a florist but a large, open rose, freshly picked from his mother's garden; a lover's rose, the colour of dark blood. Unfortunately, being home grown, it came complete with a resident earwig that fell out into her cleavage, making her shriek. She shook it out and Daniel brushed it away, breaking the tension between them and making them both laugh.

'Come on,' he said, taking command of her luggage and leading her towards his car. 'It's a bit early in the day for champagne but I know a café that makes the best coffee in Melbourne.'

'There are dozens of cafés that make the

best coffee in Melbourne,' she smiled. 'But I'm willing to give yours a try.'

Free of the air-conditioned atmosphere of the airport, Jane breathed deeply, savouring the familiar smells of home: the rain-washed eucalypt and the heady sweetness of acacia which seemed to be everywhere with its bright yellow blossom at this time of year. The air was deliciously fresh and cool. Melbourne's winter was a pleasant, well-kept secret. Unless it was actually raining or there was a cold wind blowing off the South Pole, winter in Victoria was comparable to a fine spring in other parts of the world. Daniel packed her luggage into the boot of his car and before she knew it, she was seated beside him in a handsome silver Mercedes and bowling along the freeway towards the city.

'I don't know why I stayed away so long,' she murmured. 'I do so love coming home.'

'Yes and we need to talk about that.' He spoke equally softly, keeping his gaze on the road. 'When we last met, I said a heap of things on that subject — things I didn't really mean — '

'I'm sure I did, too.' She tried to cut short his apology, knowing how much it cost him to give it. Her own temper sometimes ran away with her and she hated having to apologize for it herself. 'Maybe we should draw a line under all that and start again?'

'Thank you,' he said. 'I'd like that.' Momentarily, he took his left hand off the wheel to clasp her own. His touch was warm, dry and felt so completely right it surprised her. The contact was there for only a moment but she felt her senses jolt, every nerve come alive. Suddenly she was no longer travel-weary or tired as she met his smile. 'It's so good to have you home.'

After leaving the freeway, he drove around to the new Docklands area where a number of cafés and restaurants had sprung up to service the nearby high-rise apartments as well as the city beyond.

'But this is wonderful even at this time of year.' She stared around in surprise at the boardwalks alongside modern buildings, designed to make the most of the harbour views. 'I didn't see any of this the last time I came home.'

'It hasn't been finished all that long. It can be rather bleak if the sun doesn't shine, but Melbourne has chosen to turn on the charm today.'

He led her into a bright, modern café where the hostess greeted him by name and seated them at a table by the window overlooking the water.

'This is amazing,' she said. 'The last time I

came past here, there was nothing but old warehouses and wharves.'

'Way to go yet,' he said. 'Some parts are still like that but give it time.'

'You have an interest in these developments?' she asked.

'Not really, just friends in high places. I have fingers in a great many pies.'

'Has your mother forgiven you for not going into practice as a vet?'

'It's still a sore point so we don't talk about it. But the skills can be useful when I'm buying a horse.'

She nodded but wasn't really listening as she glanced at her watch. 'Daniel, thanks for the coffee but I really should be getting home. I haven't seen Mum yet and I really don't know what I'm going to find.'

'I understand. But I'd like to spend some time with you, Foxie. When you're more settled.'

She stared into the dregs of her coffee, thinking for a moment before she spoke. 'I don't know, Daniel. You have . . . other interests and I don't think we can just take up where we left off. And the last I heard, you were involved with some French girl?' she blurted, thinking it best to ask the direct question although the words almost choked her. 'And getting quite serious, Mum said.'

She paused with an enquiring glance, waiting for him to elaborate.

'Suzie.' He shrugged, staring into his own empty cup. 'History, I'm afraid. Old news. The bird has flown — all the way back to France.'

'Oh Daniel, I'm so sorry,' she said, keeping a sympathetic look on her face although her rogue heart was leaping for joy at this news. 'Were you very upset?'

To her surprise, he laughed aloud. 'For an actress, Foxie, you're not very good at hiding your feelings.'

'And what do you mean by that?'

'Nothing.' He continued to smile at her as if she'd said something that delighted him. 'I don't upset easily, that's all.' He glanced at his watch. 'And if you've finished your coffee, I'll take you home. Long as my car isn't on its knees, carrying all that luggage of yours.'

2

As Daniel took a meandering route through the bayside suburbs instead of bowling down the motorway to take her home, Foxie enjoyed seeing familiar landmarks on the way. St Kilda with its huge palm trees and the gaping carnival mask of Luna Park giving it a holiday atmosphere, even on a working day. Then Brighton and Sandringham with the trees bent low by the winds across wide, green lawns. The historic old clock at Black Rock.

Daniel chatted about his various projects on the way; a set of units he had put up the money to build, a fitness complex and a shopping strip where he owned several stores.

'But most of these projects seem to be finished,' she observed. 'What are you working on now?'

He fell silent for a moment, as if her question had caught him off guard. 'Foxie, this isn't the time,' he said at last. 'I don't like discussing important stuff when I'm driving. Too easy to lose concentration and have an accident.'

'OK.' She shrugged, feeling snubbed. 'I

didn't mean to pry.'

'Honestly, you're not. I didn't mean — '

'I said it's OK.' She stared out of the window, no longer quite so happy with the day. 'I was only making conversation, anyway.'

He took a deep breath, sensing her change in mood. 'Look Foxie, there are several changes you don't know about yet — '

'What sort of changes?' His tone set alarm bells ringing in her mind.

'It's complicated and I can't spare the time to get into it, not right now.'

'Fine.' Foxie's temper flared. 'I'm sure you think I'm just a ditz who doesn't know about anything except acting but you couldn't be more wrong. My father spent a lot of time schooling me until I knew almost as much about the horse-racing business as he did. He always intended me to be his heir. Otherwise he wouldn't have left the business to *me*.'

Briefly Daniel took his eyes off the road to give her a startled glance. It pleased her to have surprised him.

'You're saying your father left the controlling interest in his business to you?' he said slowly as if letting the words sink in.

'Is that so strange to you?' She compressed her lips as a twinge of emotion caught her unawares. 'We talked about it before he died.'

'Did he actually say that? In his will?'

'I suppose so. Obviously, I don't know for sure without seeing the lawyers. But that was his intention — yes.' Foxie was satisfied to see Daniel caught on the wrong foot for once, completely taken aback. 'I didn't walk out on a lucrative job in America to come home and loll about doing nothing. I'm here to take charge of the stables and keep my father's traditions alive.'

'But you don't even hold a trainer's licence. And it takes years to get one, believe me, I know.'

'Our stable foreman, Jim Coney has one. He's held a trainer's licence for years.'

'That's all very well. But what if he decides to leave and go into business for himself?'

'What if, what if,' she mocked, irritated with him for presenting so many obstacles. 'I don't know, Daniel, I haven't thought that far ahead. And, anyway, why should Jim want to leave us? He's well paid and has comfortable quarters that go with the job.'

Daniel shrugged, having nothing further to say. She didn't know how it had happened but somehow they were no longer at ease with one another and she wasn't sure why. Maybe she was annoyed with him for being surprised that her father had left her in charge of his business. Well, she'd soon let him see that he wasn't the only showman in town, that she too was capable of becoming an entrepreneur.

Somehow her pleasure in her homecoming had evaporated and sensing she wasn't in the mood for any more sightseeing, Daniel swung the car away from the beach road and took a short cut to the motorway. In no time at all, it seemed, they were turning from the highway to take the bumpy, winding private drive that led to her parents' property on the coast.

The house was old but sound, built of local stone by her grandparents as a country retreat at a time when such properties were within the reach of an average family and didn't command the six figure sums of today. Her father had added an extra wing and the racing stables during the seventies, bringing in a string of racehorses to train at the local track. His stables were modest in size, not large enough to compete with the high profile city trainers, but his horses did well in the country and he had brought in the occasional winner in town.

Inevitably, as soon as some clients heard of John Marlowe's terminal illness, they took their horses away to be trained elsewhere but most of the people they valued were loyal, or so Foxie believed.

At last the ranch-style homestead came in

view, bringing unexpected tears to her eyes. How would it feel to be home when it no longer contained the father she loved? Although, at first glance, it all looked the same, subtle changes were already taking place. When they pulled up outside the back door, the house seemed oddly calm and silent. In her father's day, there would have been constant activity: a row of cars parked haphazardly in the driveway and informal visitors standing around in the kitchen drinking the strong tea her mother provided from dawn until dusk. Owners discussing the preparation and progress of their horses, jockeys and even rival trainers. The unexpected silence brought home the loss of her father more than anything else so far and her eyes swam with tears as Daniel unloaded her cases, pretending not to see.

'You'll come in?' she said unsteadily. 'Have some tea or coffee before you drive back to town?'

'I don't think so, Foxie. Not now,' he said with surprising gentleness. 'You'll want to see the folks on your own and start settling in. But we do need to talk — and soon.' Before she realized what he would do, he pulled her into his arms, brushed away her tears with his fingers before kissing her gently but firmly on the lips.

Now Foxie was no stranger to kisses. In the course of filming *The Brave and the Free* she had stretched across many a bed, appearing to kiss dozens of handsome young men. But there had always been camera angles and other technicalities to consider. The faces of both actors had to be visible to the camera at all times. And although kisses had to seem genuine, they were never distracting. Care must be taken not to smudge lipstick or make-up.

Daniel's kiss wasn't like that at all. It was spontaneous, efficient, enthusiastic without being invasive, yet intense enough to leave her unexpectedly trembling and, impossibly, longing for more. And it took her so completely by surprise, she could think of nothing to say. As she stood there, staring at him, bracing her knees to stop them from shaking, he gave her a cheeky grin and a gentle tap on the shoulder before he returned to his car and drove swiftly away, churning the gravel behind him as he went.

Not wanting him to know just how much his kiss had unsettled her, Foxie deliberately scrubbed her lips on the back of her hand to wipe the memory of it away. She could only hope he was watching her in the rear view mirror.

Daniel saw the childish gesture and

laughed aloud, winding down the window to give her a jaunty salute.

When she turned back to the house she saw the back door had opened and her father's older sister, Jo, stood framed in the doorway, hands on hips, her miniature Yorkshire terrier bouncing up and down beside her, barking its head off. Foxie winced. It was a spoilt, evil little dog and she had always hated it. No wonder there was no sign of her father's old greyhound, Witherspoon, who usually came running out to greet her, tail gently wagging. Sensibly, the old dog must have taken refuge in the stables.

Tall and dark haired like her younger brother, Jo had many of the same family mannerisms and almost the same tone of voice. But there the similarities came to an end. Jo lacked her brother's cheerful, optimistic view of life, tending to be gloomy and suspicious of anyone's good intentions. Foxie couldn't help wondering why she was here. Who had sent for her? Jo was the last person her mother needed at such a testing time.

'So you're home, are you?' Jo stated the obvious, offering a dry cheek to be kissed. 'About time, too. What kept you? Your plane was supposed to get in around nine?'

'It did.' Foxie offered no further explanation, making a mental note to scoot Aunty Jo back home at the first opportunity. Although her heart was in the right place and her intentions basically good, she couldn't open her mouth without making it sound like a criticism.

'Was that Daniel brought you home? Why didn't he come in? I made enough lunch for four — my famous cock-a-leekie stew,' she said proudly. Foxie closed her eyes, suppressing a smile. Jo didn't know how to cook anything but an old fowl, boiled off its bones, together with leeks and rice. Daniel had had a lucky escape.

'Too busy.' Foxie shrugged. 'Said he'd leave me to settle in.'

Jo almost snorted. 'As if you need to settle into your own home.' She picked up the smallest of Foxie's cases, leaving her to struggle with the rest, eyeing the green linen suit, no longer as crisp as when it started out. 'Isn't that a bit New York for down here in the country — ?'

'I'll change as soon as I can get something unpacked.' Foxie cut across what looked like developing into a new stream of criticism. Jo was renowned for it. 'So where's Mum?' She peered past her aunt, looking into the kitchen. 'Is she OK?'

'Still in bed, I expect.'

'In bed? But it's nearly lunch time. She isn't ill?'

'Not so much ill as depressed.' Jo pulled a face. 'And I don't know how to jolly her out of it. I've told her it's time she bucked herself up and joined the land of the living. It isn't as if John's death was all that unexpected. She knew it was going to happen and had plenty of time to get used to it.'

Not trusting herself to reply to these callous remarks, Foxie made for the stairs, running up two at a time.

'She's probably still asleep,' Jo called after her. 'The doc gave her some pretty hefty sleeping pills.'

On the landing, Foxie turned, glaring down at her.

'She doesn't need sleeping pills — she needs love, understanding and plenty of fresh air.'

'Oh, so we're a medical expert now, are we?' Jo muttered, retreating to the kitchen to check on her casserole, boiling furiously on the Aga. 'Beastly old-fashioned stove,' she grumbled, scraping the bottom of the pot as she saw the leeks were sticking to the sides and the rice was in danger of catching. 'Can't control the heat.'

Upstairs, Foxie knocked gently on her

mother's bedroom door and, hearing no answer, quietly opened it and went in. The room was hot, stuffy and shrouded in darkness, the curtains still drawn as if it were the middle of the night. Marion was indeed still in bed, not asleep but hugging the pillow to stifle the sound of her weeping. Foxie sat on the bed beside her and gently placed a hand on her shoulder.

'Go away, Jo,' her mother said. 'I don't want any lunch.'

'It's not Jo,' Foxie whispered. Immediately, her mother turned and when she saw who it was, pulled her daughter into a fierce embrace.

'Oh Foxie, darling! You're here at last. You're home.'

'Yes I am. And from now on things are going to change around here. Firstly, I'm getting you out of that bed and into some clothes. You're coming downstairs.' Foxie threw open the drapes and opened the window to let in some cool, fresh air.

'Oh darling, I can't.' Marion found a box of tissues and grabbed a handful to blow her nose. 'Jo hates to see me in tears.'

'Then she can get over it. You have every right to express your grief.' And, as if the mention of it unlocked her own suppressed tears, Foxie embraced her mother again and they wept together, comforting each other.

A few minutes later, Jo called up the stairs, making them both flinch. 'Are you two coming down to lunch before this wretched stew boils away?'

'Oh dear,' Marion whispered, shaking her head. 'I don't know if I can face any more of Jo's burnt chicken stew.'

'Be brave.' Foxie took a tissue before handing the box to her mother. 'By this time tomorrow, Jo and her mean little dog will be on their way. Earlier still if I have anything to do with it.'

'Foxie, she's family. Your father's last living relative. We can't possibly ask her to leave.'

'Just watch me. And don't worry, I shall be tactful. She'll think she's decided it all on her own.'

'She's been so good, really. I don't want to hurt her feelings.'

'It'll be OK. I have a plan. You know how paranoid she is about germs? I'll tell her I'm coming down with a gastric flu, picked up before leaving LA. Nothing worse than flu in a hot climate.' Foxie pretended to test her forehead with the back of her hand. 'They're dropping like flies over there. Hospitals overflowing.'

The plan worked. Aunty Jo could scarcely wait to finish her lunch before bundling her belongings and her terrier into her ram-shackle old Volvo.

'I do hope you'll manage without me, Marion.' She gave Foxie's mother a quick embrace and was about to kiss Foxie until she remembered herself and recoiled. 'But I can't risk anything gastric, not with my delicate stomach. I hope you'll feel better soon, Foxie, but you really shouldn't have travelled, spreading disease.' Still muttering to herself, she started up her old Volvo which coughed a few times before rumbling unwillingly to life, allowing her to drive it away.

'I can't believe you did that,' Marion giggled, still waving as the Volvo disappeared, bouncing and lurching down the drive. 'We really will have to do something about remaking that road. Maybe Daniel will — '

'Daniel? What does he have to do with it?' Foxie said more sharply than she intended. 'And if you and Rose have been matchmaking again, you can forget it. I came back home to make myself useful, not to get married to Daniel.'

'Of course not, dear,' Marion said meekly, keeping her expression bland. 'Nobody ever said you did.'

After clearing away the remains of Jo's unfortunate stew, Foxie changed into a pair of old jeans and a jumper. She now realized that with this complete change of lifestyle, she was going to need an entirely new wardrobe. Clothes that were so right in LA seemed totally out of place in country Victoria. And, at this time of year, she would need warm jackets and raincoats for early mornings with the horses. Because, although her father thought well of Jim Coney, trusting his judgement and treating him almost as one of the family, she had no intention of letting him make all the decisions, trainer's licence or no.

Before visiting the stables, she made her way to the back paddock to see the old faithfuls enjoying their well-earned retirement. Her father kept as many as he could and she recognized most of them but when she arrived at the fence, she was surprised to see Jim Coney there before her, counting them, a speculative look on his face.

'Hi, Jim,' she greeted him warmly with a hug. 'I was just on my way to see you but I thought I'd check out the pensioners first.'

'There are so many of them,' Jim sighed. 'And they eat as much as if they were still in work. Your father never could bear to part with a useless horse.'

'And neither shall I,' Foxie said firmly, tossing her head and leaning back against the fence as if protecting them from Jim's critical eye. 'They've earned their retirement.'

'Wouldn't matter so much if we could afford it, Miss Marlowe,' Jim muttered, scratching his chin. An old jockey who had ridden professionally until he was well into his forties, he had one of those long, deeply lined faces that never filled out, giving him a permanently mournful expression. 'We've lost more than one high profile owner lately an' now we'll have to cut our suit according to the cloth.'

'And what does that mean?'

'To put it plainly, some of these old dears have to go.'

'Over my dead body. My father would turn in his grave.'

'An' there's more than old horses to worry about. There's wages an' bills to be paid. Mr Morgan's been very good, comin' to the rescue like he did, but even he hasn't got a bottomless pit of money.'

'Daniel Morgan? Why on earth should we need to borrow money from him?'

'Borrow?' Jim stared at her for a moment. 'Oh, Lor' — Mrs Marlowe hasn't told you, has she? She's been gettin' that forgetful lately.'

'Told me what? So far you've done nothing but talk in riddles, Jim, and I'm getting tired of it.'

The foreman's expression became more

hangdog than ever. 'I'm thinkin' I'd better come on up to the house. Thrash it out like we always do — over a nice cup of tea.'

★   ★   ★

Foxie did her best to stay calm while Jim and her mother tried to explain their reasons for allowing John Marlowe's racing stables to be bought out and taken over by Daniel Morgan Enterprises. As soon as he could see Foxie had grasped the facts, Jim excused himself to go back to the stables, realizing that mother and daughter needed to talk alone.

'Thanks for the tea,' he said unnecessarily, relieved to be making his escape.

As soon as Jim was out of earshot, Foxie stood up and started pacing the room, working herself into a temper.

'What a mess,' she raged. 'Selling us out to Morgan the pirate. Oh, Mum, how could you? You might at least have waited till I came home.'

'But I thought you *liked* Daniel. You were inseparable a few years ago — '

'That was then,' Foxie said dismissively, folding her arms and glaring at Marion.

'Well, I'm sorry if it's come as a shock but I had to do *something*. You don't understand how it was.' Her mother searched for words, twisting her hands in her lap. 'During the last six months of your father's life, when people began to realize that — that he wouldn't be there any more . . . ' she took a shuddering breath. 'They came up with all kinds of excuses: they must protect their investment, they were sorry but they couldn't let sentiment cloud their judgement, and more of the same. In real terms it meant that more than half of them took their horses away.'

'Even before Dad was gone? Are you telling me he had to sit here watching his business fall away?'

'Broke my heart to see him like that.' Marion paused and looked down at her lap, unable to speak for several moments. When she did, her voice was no more than a croak. 'So when Daniel offered to take over and buy it, it seemed like a godsend. The best thing for everyone.'

'Why on earth didn't you call me? I would have helped.'

'You, dear?' Her mother looked up and smiled indulgently as if Foxie were a child, offering the contents of her money box. 'But how? Your father always said actors never have any money — '

Foxie made a gesture of impatience. 'And most of them don't if they're out of work half the time. But I was in regular work for ten years — the star of the show, no less. Paid in American dollars, too.'

'Ohh!' Marion sighed, biting her lip. 'So you do have some savings? Money of your own?'

Foxie drew a deep breath, stifling her impatience. She knew how hard it was for a woman like her mother, who had left all financial affairs to her husband, to grasp the concept of a woman having substantial amounts of money to manage alone.

'But the house is still ours,' Marion brightened, pleased to have remembered something positive. 'Daniel doesn't own that.'

'And what's the good of keeping the house without an income to support it?' Foxie muttered, making Marion slump in her seat again. 'How much did Daniel pay you? Maybe he'll let me buy it back? After all, it's only another business venture to him.'

'I don't know, dear. There were a lot of overdue bills and taxes. I don't suppose there's very much left.'

'Don't you *know*?'

Marion shook her head. 'Your father always dealt with the bank and the tax people. I never had anything to do with them.'

Foxie ran her hands through her hair. 'No wonder Daniel said we had things to discuss. He must have known I'd go ballistic when I found out. This is nothing short of daylight robbery. Wait till I see him.'

'Now Foxie hold on — don't go losing your temper. He's been very good, very kind.'

'I'm sure! Paying a pittance to snatch a widow's livelihood from under her nose. He's probably a slum landlord, as well.'

'And I'm quite sure he's nothing of the sort. Far as I can see, he's behaved very fairly, very honourably.' Marion glanced at the grandmother clock which was just striking five. 'In any case, it's too late for you to go haring back to Melbourne to tackle him now. You must be exhausted after your journey, anyway. Sleep on it and you may see things more clearly in the morning.'

'More clearly maybe.' Foxie's expression was grim. 'But I doubt if I'll see them differently.'

Having slept only fitfully, Foxie rose early and made a breakfast of eggs on toast to compensate for her lack of sleep. She brewed fresh coffee and took a cup to her mother before setting off for town.

'You're a morning person just like your father,' her mother groaned. 'I've never understood folk who can face breakfast at dawn.'

'Is it all right if I take one of the cars?'

'Of course.' Sleepily, Marion groped for

44

some keys in the drawer of the bedside table and tossed them to Foxie. 'Take your father's old Holden — it could do with the run.'

As reliable and responsive as she found the old family wagon, she missed the sporty little red Porsche she had owned in LA and promised herself she would buy another as soon as time and money permitted. She had absolutely no idea how much it might cost to pay Daniel off and reclaim her inheritance but she was determined to thrash it out with him today.

Rather than make an appointment that could be broken, she chose to rely on the element of surprise. While talking to Daniel the previous day, she gained the impression that his working day started well before 9 a.m. Like most modem businessmen, he went to his offices early to check overnight e-mails and plan the day's work ahead. With any luck, she might catch him before most of his staff came in, which would be just as well if things deteriorated into a slanging match between them.

Arriving in town well before rush hour, she left the Holden in a multi-storey car park and made her way to the impressive Southbank offices of Morgan Enterprises. It was a good thing he had pointed them out to her yesterday.

She passed through revolving doors into carpeted, air-conditioned comfort with original paintings of river and seascapes on neutrally painted walls. This early, no one was yet at reception, so she checked the notice-board by the lift until she saw *Daniel Morgan, CEO — Suite 16, First Floor.*

Rather than wait for the lift, she ran up the stairs, hoping she had guessed right and that Daniel would be there. She knocked on the door of Suite 16, surprised to hear a female voice inviting her to come in.

Seated at a computer station with a reception desk beside her was a diminutive but very business-like blonde, dressed in the inevitable Melbourne business black, her long, platinum-tinted hair caught into a tidy coil on top of her head. She greeted Foxie with a warm but professional smile.

'Can I help you?' She glanced towards the inner door. 'I'm afraid Mr Morgan is busy. He doesn't see anyone until after ten. But if you'd like to leave your card, we'll get back to you.'

'Oh, I think he'll see me,' Foxie muttered and strode towards the door, only to pause in surprise as the diminutive person sprang up and stood in front her, arms outstretched to prevent her.

'I'm sorry but I can't let you in. It's a

company rule — more than my job's worth.'

Foxie regarded her, hands on hips, hoping she wouldn't have to wrestle the tiny secretary out of her path. 'And I'm sorry too but I didn't come all the way from Mornington to wait until ten o'clock.'

'Mr Morgan can't see you then, either. He has overseas visitors due at that time.'

'Then he'll just have to see me now, won't he?' Foxie realized she was raising her voice.

'But — '

At that moment, the door to the inner office opened, revealing Daniel wearing a white shirt and business trousers, his tie, not yet fastened, hanging loosely around his neck.

'Pepper, what's all the commotion? I can't hear myself think in there.' He caught sight of Foxie and took a deep breath. 'Ah, Foxie, it's you. I was wondering how long it would take.'

'You could have saved us both a lot of a trouble by telling me yesterday. Why didn't you?' She wasted no time with preliminaries, feeling all the more irritated that Daniel should look so debonair first thing in the morning while she must look hollow-eyed from jet lag and lack of sleep.

'I'm sorry, Daniel,' Pepper was biting her lip, thinking she would be blamed for the disturbance Foxie was causing. 'But I did try to tell her.'

'It's OK, Pep.' He rested a kindly hand on the girl's shoulder. 'Miss Marlowe — Foxie — happens to be an old friend.'

'A personal friend?' Pepper looked at Foxie under her brows and blushed, not liking this news any better. 'I see. That's all right, then. But she should have said.'

Daniel held open the door of his office, allowing Foxie to precede him. While the outer office had no natural light, Daniel's room, although not large, had a picture window overlooking the Yarra River and its traffic with a backdrop of the city beyond. In other circumstances, Foxie would have been entranced by the view but today she had other things on her mind.

On the wall behind Daniel's desk was a seascape, showing a three-masted clipper, struggling through mountainous waves. He saw her glance at it.

'I keep it as a reminder of how our forefathers did it tough,' he said.

'But Daniel, why didn't you — ?' In no mood for small talk, she tried to come straight to the point.

'Sit down and make yourself comfortable first. You look all in. Coffee?'

She was considering refusing until she

reminded herself she would need all her wits about her.

'Thanks.' She eased herself into the visitor's chair placed opposite his desk, interested to see that he was preparing the coffee himself rather than phone through an order to Pepper.

'Milk and no sugar?' he asked, smiling at her. 'You see I remember.'

'Daniel, if you wanted a racing stables, there must have been more than one on the market. Why did you have to take ours?'

'Just a minute, Foxie, let's get something straight here. You seem to have the impression I've done something wrong?'

'Haven't you? Taking advantage of — '

'I haven't taken advantage of anyone. I bought your father's stables because my mother asked me to, rather than let them fall into unfriendly hands. Boulters were already sniffing around — they've wanted a foothold in Victoria for some time. Our mothers are very old friends — I don't need to tell you that. They knew I had some ideas for improvement, ideas that might turn the business around.'

'Why should it need turning around? My father ran those stables successfully for more than thirty years.'

'Until he got sick. And because his business

relied so completely on his own talent and personality, that's when things started to go wrong.'

'Hah! And you couldn't wait to snap up the bargain, could you?'

'Foxie, it wasn't like that.'

'How was it then, Daniel?' She drained her coffee cup and sat back, regarding him. 'You tell me.'

Daniel also sat back, staring back at her. How could he tell her of the terrible mess he had found on taking over the business? The books that hadn't been properly kept for years, the overdue taxes and escalating fines for late payment, the accountants who had shrugged their shoulders and given up when they weren't paid. It had taken Daniel's own accountants a month to make sense out of any of it. And here was Foxie, taking him to task as if he were some kind of corporate raider.

'Tell me what you paid to my mother and I'll buy it back — with interest obviously, to make it worth your while.'

He stared at her, thinking how amazingly young and vulnerable she looked this morning, eyes shining and her skin glowing with the intensity of emotion. He looked away, reminding himself he shouldn't get sidetracked; her long-legged, natural style of beauty was a trap in which he'd been caught before. Not having seen her for several years before being commandeered to meet her at the airport, he had expected to bury the hatchet and establish a friendly relationship — nothing more. It was a shock to realize he still had feelings for her, no matter how deeply buried.

'I'd like an answer to my question.' She was getting impatient. 'What do you say?'

'Let me ask you something before I do. Exactly how much money do you think you'll need to buy me out?'

'Oh no, I'm not falling for that one. You name your price and I'll see if I can match it.'

He shrugged, spreading his hands. 'How long is a piece of string?'

Temper rising, she pushed back her chair and stood up. 'That does it. I came here to make you a genuine business offer but if you're not prepared to take it seriously — '

'Foxie believe me, I take all this very seriously. Which is why I'd like you to sit down and answer my questions.' He waited until she sat down again on the edge of her seat, regarding him warily. 'If you were indeed able to buy it back, what would you do with your father's business?'

'Run it, of course, the way that he always did.'

'In exactly the same way?'

'Why not?' She was beginning to feel uneasy, less sure of herself. 'What are you getting at?'

'Because you'd have only half the business he had before. And I don't think people will be falling over themselves to bring horses to be trained by an old jockey and an ex soapstar.'

'And they *will* bring their horses to Daniel Morgan, the pirate?'

'Ouch!' he said. 'You do have a terrible opinion of me, don't you?'

'I've not even started to tell you what I think.'

'Save it. I'm probably all that you think and more but even I wouldn't cheat my mother's oldest friend.'

'So you will let me buy it back?'

'Do you have one and a half million dollars?'

'Don't be ridiculous.' Foxie felt the colour drain from her face. 'My mother said you had to pay some bills and late taxes but father's little racing stables have never been worth that kind of money.'

'Don't I know it. But that's the total of what I need to invest to turn them into a viable busiuness.'

'And exactly how do you propose to do that?'

'Finally,' he grinned at her. 'I thought you'd never ask.'

3

She continued regarding him with suspicion and he sighed, looking at the small lines of ill temper gathering between her brows.

'Lets make something clear,' he said softly. 'I don't want to fight with you, Foxie. I want to work with you.'

'Oh? And what makes you think I'd want to work for *you*?'

'Not *for* me; I said *with* me. Together, we could make the Marlowe Racing Stables really count for something. Combine our talents. I know what to look for in buying a horse; you and Jim know how to train them.'

'Yes, but you'd own everything and still be in charge,' she remarked, unwilling to be gracious.

'I see this as a partnership. Aren't you just a little bit curious to know what I have in mind?'

'Go on then, impress me.' She folded her arms, sat back and waited for him to do so.

'Instead of taking horses to train for private owners, we will buy promising 2-year-olds and sell shares in a syndicate. I've seen quite a few trainers doing it these days. It brings ownership within the reach of the average racing enthusiast — six to ten people can share ownership of a horse. For a small initial investment and a modest retainer, they can have the full race-day experience as an owner and the thrill of accepting the prize if the horse should win — '

'Yet you retain the controlling interest.' In spite of herself, Foxie was intrigued. 'But don't you have to have a dealer's licence to sell syndicate shares?'

'Not necessarily. Most of our business will come through word of mouth.'

'Yes, but what happens if somebody wants to drop out?'

'Their share would be offered to the other members of the syndicate first. Dropouts aren't usually a problem if you have a successful horse.'

'Ah, but if you don't?'

'Most of my horses are.' Daniel was confident. 'Look at my record.'

'Don't you worry, I will. And where exactly do I fit into the scheme of things?'

'As your father's daughter, for a start, carrying on his traditions. Your fame on the small screen won't go amiss, either.'

'That's not what you said before.'

'I was too hasty. I know lots of women who'd like to boast that Carole Parker was training her horse.'

'So you *have* watched *The Brave and the Free*,' Foxie laughed, enjoying catching him out. 'Or how would you know that — '

'Don't flatter yourself. There's almost as much in the gossip columns about Carole Parker as there is about you.'

'You're a closet soap-fan,' she accused.

'OK, OK. But don't tell Pepper or I'll never heard the end of it.'

She smiled. A few years ago, Daniel would have died rather than admit to watching something he defined as 'candyfloss for the mind'. He changed the subject, wanting to get back to the business in hand.

'Yesterday, Foxie, you caught me by surprise. Marion never mentioned that you expected your father to leave his business to you.'

'I'm afraid my mother marches to a different tune. Business has never been high on her list of priorities. She would have been grateful to wash her hands of it and turn it all over to you.'

'Well, she never said anything of your expectations to Rose or to me. No wonder my takeover came as rather a shock.'

'That's an understatement,' she muttered.

'All the same, I believe it can work out well for both of us. My accountants have drawn up a projection over the next twelve months and if you decide to join me in equal partnership, you can invest — '

'Invest? Hold on a moment. Now you're saying I have to buy a partnership in what should have been mine by right — '

'Foxie, I don't think you appreciate how bad the situation was. If I hadn't stepped in when I did, Marlowe's Racing Stables would no longer exist.'

'What?' She blinked at him, stunned by this news.

'Boulter Brothers have been wanting a foothold in Melbourne for years and Marion told me they were already sniffing around. They'd have snapped up Marlowe's for a pittance while it was on its knees and it would have been part of Boulter Brothers' Melbourne operation even before you got back from LA. Their next step would have been to put pressure on Marion to sell them the house and that would have been the end of it. You wouldn't have been offered partnership with *them*.'

Foxie sat back, stunned by this blunt assessment of the situation. 'So you expect me to be grateful for your intervention?'

Daniel sighed. 'I don't expect anything from you, Foxie. I'm just telling it like it is. But since you're interested and concerned enough to come hunting me up at this hour, you deserve to know the truth. I can see how strongly you feel about your father's business.'

'Of course I do. It's my heritage.'

'OK, then. Look, I'm not the bad guy here. We're on the same side and I'd really like you to be part of the team.'

'Thanks,' she said in a small voice. 'I'm sorry, Daniel. I read you wrong. We have a talent for misunderstanding each other, don't we? I had no idea things were that bad. It's all come as rather a shock.'

'I'm sure. It just needed a bit more communication, that's all.' He smiled. 'Have dinner with me tonight and we'll talk some more.'

'I don't know. I wasn't planning on staying in town all day. My mother's really not — '

'Now don't you worry about Marion. I'll get Mum to call her and take her out to lunch.'

'Would you? I do need to do some shopping: I'm in desperate need of some clothes.'

'You go shopping, then. And while you're at it, find something pretty to wear tonight.'

'Not just the old bistro by the beach, then?'

'No. This is a celebration. I'll get Pepper to get us a table at the best place in town.'

The dull early morning had given way to a lovely, sunny day and when Foxie left Daniel's office, people were seated drinking coffee at the riverside cafés, the pleasure boats already plying their trade on the river. Her heart lifted at the thought of having a whole day to spend pampering and indulging herself.

Before going shopping, she dropped into a spa for a massage and a pedicure. Then she went to the hairdresser she always visited when she was in town.

'Foxie!' Vince greeted her with a hug as soon as she entered the salon. A big man with a beard and shock of curly hair, he looked more like a truck driver than a hair-stylist but he was a genius with colour and wielded his scissors with a touch like magic. 'Oh dear.' He pulled a face as he examined the reddish locks, curling limply past her shoulders. 'What's happened here? Those TV stylists have much to answer for.'

'To say nothing of jet lag,' she explained briefly. 'And on top of that, I've just come from the spa.'

'Why don't we do a total makeover?' He grinned at her in the mirror. 'Let Carole Parker go strawberry blonde?'

'Vince, I haven't told you. I'm not playing Carole Parker any more — '

'What? They can't have sacked you from *The Brave and the Free*?' Vince rested his hands on her shoulders to stare at her in the mirror. 'That's not fair. I only watch it to see you.'

'I didn't renew my contract, that's all.' She smiled back at him. 'I decided ten years was enough and I should get out before they turned me into a grandma.'

'Grandma? You? You're not even thirty.'

'People age quickly in soap-land.'

'So what are we going to do?' Vince returned to the subject of her hair. 'It'll gain body and bring back the condition if we cut a fair bit off.' He lifted her streak of white hair with the tip of his comb. 'And isn't it time you let me get rid of this?'

'No, because it'll only come back.' Foxie grinned at him in the mirror. 'But you can darken the red and put in a few highlights, if you like.'

'OK.' Vince gave in with a sigh and lifted the distinctive streak clear while he went to work on the rest of her head. An hour or so later, her red hair vibrant again, fashionably streaked and trimmed into a bouncy, shorter style, Foxie parted company with her stylist, promising not to leave it too long before she saw him again.

She visited a department store and bought jackets and jeans as well as several pretty sweaters for everyday life in the country, but she couldn't find that extra special dress she needed for the evening ahead. After returning her purchases to the car, now parked under the new shopping complex at Melbourne Central, she decided to start again, having a sudden fancy for something unusual. Not that she cared about impressing Daniel Morgan — no, of course not. She wanted something glamorous and special, solely to please herself.

She looked in the stores of several local designers and had she wanted a sophisticated 'little black dress' or a glittering evening top to wear with a black velvet skirt, she could have been satisfied in minutes. But she wanted to find something amazing, rather than something that would merely 'do'.

Finally, she remembered a shop she had visited once in one of the city's many arcades. She had been looking for a handbag at the time and was delighted with the vintage snakeskin purse she found there. The shop was an eclectic mixture of classical vintage items together with a unique range of clothing and accessories the owners imported from Hong Kong. But which arcade? For the moment, she couldn't remember except she felt sure it was somewhere off Collins Street.

She progressed through Block Arcade and bought the hand-made chocolates that her mother loved but there was still no sign of the shop she remembered. After crossing Collins Street and walking through Centreway Arcade, she began to lose heart. Five more minutes and she'd be at Flinders Street Station. Then she saw it, the window filled with glittering golden handbags, exotic high-heeled shoes and vintage plastic jewellery, bright and tempting as freshly made sweets. Inside, there were teenaged students trying on kinky, green-spotted boots. Foxie hesitated in the doorway, suddenly daunted. Was she too old for all this? Should she go back to the department store and buy herself that conventional little black dress? The shop assistant's welcome decided her; a girl with a mop of red hair, not all that different from her own.

'This shop is amazing, isn't it?' the girl enthused. 'And you've come on the right day, too. We've just been putting out the latest shipment from Hong Kong. Looking for something special, are you?'

Foxie smiled back at her. 'I was hoping to find a rather special dress.'

61

'Then you've come to the right place. Is it an eighties party or — '

'No. Just a dinner date but I wanted — '

'To really knock his eye out, yes?'

'Yes, but nothing too — '

'Obvious. I know.' The girl let Foxie know they were on the same wavelength.

Half an hour later, Foxie was the proud possessor of a pair of strappy gold sandals and a little Venetian gold leather evening purse to match but still hadn't found *the* dress. The problem, as she had often discovered before, was her height.

'Sometimes, I think it's worse than being too short.' She sighed as she paid for the shoes and bag, thanking the helpful assistant for her time.

'And you do have your heart set on vintage?' the girl asked.

'I just don't like modern, synthetic fabrics,' Foxie explained.

'There is another shop here in town. It's only tiny but she sometimes has beautiful things.'

Minutes later, Foxie was striding back towards Bourke Street, following directions to the shop in Royal Arcade. In the window was exactly what she was looking for — not a dress, but a beautiful 1930s silk velvet black evening-coat. She couldn't wait to try it on.

'It swamps most people because it's so long, but that shouldn't be a problem for you.' The young shop assistant, who was tall herself, noticed Foxie's height. Foxie slid into the coat, enjoying the feel of the pure silk lining against her skin. Although it had to be more than sixty years old, it had been treasured and well kept, the silk velvet as vibrant as when it was made. Wide sleeves fell as far as the elbow and then fastened with many buttons, tapering to the wrist. It had a wide, flattering collar to frame the face, perfect with Foxie's newly bobbed short hair, and it fastened with a vintage marcasite clasp on one hip. She came out of the changing room, making the shop assistant gasp in genuine pleasure.

'It could have been made for you,' she said.

'What do I wear underneath?'

'Chanel No.5?' the girl joked. 'No, seriously, a garment like this can double as either a coat or dress, but I have a black silk petticoat to go with it if you like?'

At five clock, purchases safely stowed in the car, it was still too early for her to join Daniel at his house in Kew. She was also hungry as she hadn't bothered with more than a cup of coffee for lunch but she didn't want to snack now in case it spoiled her appetite for the meal ahead. Hunger always made her bad-tempered so she hoped Daniel had chosen a restaurant in or near the city. Having well over an hour to kill before meeting him, she collected the car and drove to look at Port Melbourne and the beach. Although the city beaches had once been despised and rejected for those further afield, with the advent of luxury accommodation nearby, local councils had spent money to clean and restore them so that the new city-dwellers could use them as playgrounds. Surprisingly, although it would soon be dark, the beach was quite busy, people braving the evening breeze off the sea as they walked their dogs, schoolboys and girls still in uniform, laughing and flirting as they walked on the pavement flanking the beach.

Foxie felt a momentary pang of guilt about Marion. What if Rose had been unable to take her to lunch? Would Daniel have told her? Maybe not. Quickly she pressed the button for *home* on her cell phone and her mother answered almost immediately. She sounded happier than she had been for some time and Foxie could hear the laughter in her voice as if she had just been sharing a joke.

'Of course I'm all right,' she said in response to her daughter's query. 'Rose and I had lunch at the pub and now she's staying here for supper with me. You go and enjoy yourself, darling. Stay overnight in town, if you like.'

'Are you trying to push me into Daniel's arms, Ma? Because if so, I can tell you right now — '

'Nothing was further from my mind!' Marion lied blatantly. 'I just don't like the thought of your driving home when you've had a few drinks.'

'Ma, listen to me.' Foxie could feel irritation rising. 'I've no idea what impression Daniel has given to Rose but this is a business meeting so far as I'm concerned — not an occasion for getting drunk.' Even as she said it, Foxie realized how uptight and prissy she sounded. Marion giggled: clearly she and Rose had been sinking a few glasses of wine themselves.

'And did you find a beautiful dress? Daniel said you were looking for one?'

Even this innocent comment struck a nerve. 'I think everyone's building a lot more on this dinner date than I am. I bought myself a black coat.'

'Oh.' Marion sounded disappointed.

'A beautiful black velvet coat.' Foxie relented.

'I'm sure you'll look gorgeous, darling.' Her mother was happy again. 'You always do. Give our love to Daniel and have a wonderful evening together.'

After cutting the connection, Foxie inspected herself in the rear-view mirror, suddenly uneasy about the evening ahead. What kind of 'partnership' was Daniel really proposing? Did he expect her to fall back into his arms and consequently his bed? She had a brief mental picture of their mothers, smiling indulgently, ready to tuck them in. Teased and irritated by such thoughts, she began to be sorry she had taken so much trouble with her appearance, in case it gave him the wrong impression. Would he think she was trying too hard? She scratched her fingers through her hair to make it look more casual but as soon as she shook it again, it bounced back into shape.

She glanced at her watch, wondering if she would have time to purchase a 'little black dress' after all but she knew that unless it was Thursday or Friday — which it wasn't — very few shops would remain open after six. To be sure, casual dress was acceptable in most places these days but she'd feel at just as much of a disadvantage if she turned up in the same crumpled clothes she'd been wearing that morning to find Daniel resplendent in a dinner suit. He had already told her it was a celebration and an occasion for dressing up. It was hardly fair to punish him for their mothers' viewpoint of this 'date'.

She made up her face and changed in the

ladies' rest-room of a city hotel, buttoning the coat so severely that the collar stood up around her face. Fortunately, at this time of year, the evening was breezy and cool.

The sight of Daniel's red-brick house in Kew brought all the memories of their time together flooding back: Daniel making dinner for her, candles and all; Daniel cosseting her with hot lemon juice and whisky when she had a cold; Daniel teasing her about her fear of spiders — a large huntsman had galloped across the ceiling while they were lying in bed, and how quickly he had put it outside when he saw she was genuinely frightened; Daniel cooking breakfast for her on Sunday morning while she read his newspapers on the patio; drinking mulled wine and watching television together on a chilly afternoon. How could everything have gone so wrong when it had all seemed to be going so right?

In the end they had both lost their tempers, saying much more than they should; hurtful things that they didn't mean and shouldn't have said. And although they had now agreed to draw a line under past mistakes, it was still hard to forget.

Daniel must have been watching and waiting for her arrival because as she parked her father's car beside his gleaming, silver Mercedes, he opened the door, the hall light

67

shining on his red hair, several shades darker than her own. Not surprisingly, her heart skipped a beat. As she locked the car and walked towards him, he gave a slow smile, taking in her appearance.

'Wow!' he said softly. 'You look wonderful, like something right out of Agatha Christie — the Queen of the Night.'

Foxie smiled, glancing at him through her eyelashes. She was wearing more make-up than usual to match the glamour of the coat.

'And you've had your hair done as well.' He looked a little less happy, seeing that it had been cut.

'I thought it was time for a change. Don't you like it?'

'I can't say it doesn't suit you, but I loved your long hair.'

'Maybe. But short hair is more suitable for my new image as a businesswoman,' she said firmly, letting him know the subject was closed. He gave her a brief kiss of greeting on the cheek and she felt an unexpected stab of desire, immediately aware of the subtle cologne he used, reminding her of their time as lovers yet again. Tonight he wasn't in a dinner-suit but was wearing a dark blue suit so immaculate she thought it was most likely Armani. She wanted to move in close and test the quality of it, running her hands up under the lapels, but she quelled the instinct immediately.

This won't do at all! She scolded herself. This is a celebration of a *business* relationship — nothing more.

'I hope you're hungry,' he said.

'Starved,' she said, trying not to think of her rumbling stomach and wishing she'd taken the time to sit down and have lunch.

'Good. And if I remember rightly, you love Chinese food?' He glanced at his watch. 'We have time for a cocktail, if you like? The taxi won't be here for another ten minutes.'

'Taxi?'

'You bet. If we're making a night of it, I don't want to have to worry about drinking and driving — '

'You don't have to. I could drive.'

He waved her objections away as he ushered her inside, found cocktail glasses and set about mixing a martini; from experience she knew it would be very dry and very strong.

'Daniel, hold on a minute. I've still got to drive home afterwards.'

'No you don't. I got my housekeeper to make up the bed in the spare room. And in case you're worried, it's at the opposite end of the house from mine.'

She was irritated to feel herself blushing at

the possibilities. 'All the same, I don't think it's a good idea. If we're to be business partners, we should keep it that way.'

'For pity's sake, what's the big deal? I'm only offering you a bed for the night. You can take yourself off to some hotel if you'd rather — '

'Maybe I will!' Her own temper flashed, matching his own.

'Cheers!' he said, slipping an olive into her martini and offering it. 'Same old Foxie, abrasive as ever. You haven't mellowed at all.' He downed his own drink before she had scarcely tasted hers and she sipped cautiously, expecting it to be strong. It was.

Rescue came in the form of the taxi driver at the door; not a normal taxi at all but a white limousine, complete with driver in uniform.

'Daniel, really.' She smiled at his extravagance. 'People will think we're getting engaged or something.' *What on earth had possessed her to say that?* Fortunately, he thought nothing of it and just grinned.

The limo driver did his best to stay poker-faced, but he was clearly knocked out by Foxie's appearance and kept glancing at her from time to time in the rear-view mirror. He was frowning slightly, aware that she was a celebrity but not quite able to place her.

In a very short time, they were bidding him farewell outside one of the most famous Chinese restaurants in Melbourne, in the Chinese quarter of Little Bourke Street. The street was narrow and the pavements small and treacherous so Foxie had to watch her step in her new high heels, but they were soon inside the colourful restaurant, decorated with huge tasselled lanterns and statues of snarling Chinese dogs. They were greeted by a beautiful Chinese hostess who seated them at one of the prime tables by the window.

She was about to leave them to study the menu when Daniel reminded her that he had called in his order ahead of them, so that they wouldn't have to wait.

Foxie wasn't surprised when he asked for champagne or rather the local equivalent, made by French wine-makers and in the traditional manner. To her relief, food arrived fairly promptly and she found herself doing justice to a wonderful selection of traditional Cantonese dishes, accompanied by a large bowl of fluffy white rice.

'You weren't joking about being starved, were you?' Daniel said.

'I got so involved with the shopping, I forgot to have lunch,' she admitted, feeling better tempered and less edgy now that her

71

stomach was full. 'That was wonderful, Daniel. The best Chinese I've ever tasted.'

'They have a reputation to keep. Now can I tempt you to a sweet?'

Before she could answer, a woman came up and stood at their table, hands on hips. She was a large lady and didn't mind being rude, peering closely into Foxie's face.

'It is you, isn't it? Carole Parker. I'd know you anywhere, in spite of the snazzy new haircut. I knew you hadn't died in that car crash, not really.' She turned to Daniel, giving him a quick look up and down. 'And up to your old tricks already, I see. Yet another new man. And there's that nice husband of yours, still waiting at home, putting up with it all these years, always taking you back — '

'Excuse me.' Foxie was trying to stem the torrent of words. 'But I don't think you — '

A fat finger jabbed Foxie in the chest. 'And what about those poor kids? Women like you never think about what it's doing to them. All you think about is your own pleasure.'

'Now just a minute, Madam.' Daniel stood up, ready to join the fray.

'Daniel, sit down,' Foxie said quietly. 'This has happened before. I can deal with it.' He did so but warily, still ready to leap to her defence. She turned to the intruder, giving her Carole Parker's warmest smile. 'And your name is?'

'Stella.'

'So Stella, you must be a long time fan of *The Brave and the Free*?'

'I've been watching what goes on for years and I've never liked *you*.'

'Stella, it isn't real life, it's only a story — an ongoing story. And I'm not really Carole Parker. My name is — '

'Don't give me that. I know who you are. I'm standing right in front of you, aren't I?'

At that moment a waiter appeared at the table. 'Is there a problem, sir? madam? Is this lady bothering you?'

Stella drew a deep breath. She had been so absorbed, she hadn't realized that she was creating a scene. 'It's all right, I'll go now,' she said, glaring at Foxie. 'But you won't get away with it. I won't forget that I've seen you.'

Foxie and Daniel said nothing, watching as she was escorted from the room and disappeared through the front door. When she had gone, they looked at each other and burst into nervous laughter.

'Does that happen often?' Daniel said.

'All the time in LA especially if I'm out with other cast members. But it's the first time it's happened here.'

'She must be insane.'

'Not really. You see if they watch every day, the characters become part of their lives. Some people find it hard to believe we're just actors and none of it's real.'

'Are you OK? She seemed rather vicious to me. Perhaps you could do with a brandy rather than sweets.'

'Go on. It takes more than the Stellas of the world to put this girl off her feed. I'd like both. And you still haven't mentioned a word about business.'

Daniel gave her a lazy smile. 'It'll keep.'

4

As it happened, they didn't talk about business at all that night. Instead, as Daniel had always intended, they spent most of the evening catching up. She discovered that he was just as happy to listen as talk, enjoying her light-hearted LA gossip and celebrity name-dropping.

'But what about you?' she said at last. 'You've let me rave on all evening and you haven't really told me anything about yourself.'

Suddenly, he seemed less than comfortable. 'There's not much to know.'

'Oh Daniel, in four years there has to be.' The wine she had been drinking had gone to her head, giving her the courage to press him. 'Tell me about Suzette.'

He looked startled. 'Whatever for? Like I said, there's not much to know. Let's say the cultural differences were too great and caused arguments. I told her we had just as many French bakeries here as in France and she said there was more to living in France than eating French bread. She was missing her family and seemed to think I'd be willing to pull up stumps and move there to live. When she found out I wasn't, she decided they mattered more than I did.'

'I'm so sorry, Daniel.'

'Well, don't be.' He seemed irritated by her concern. 'It was early days, anyway. A kind of holiday romance. To be honest, we didn't know each other well enough to be really attached.'

'Oh?' she said softly. 'I didn't know there was a set time for something like that.'

'Far as I'm concerned, it's a closed book.' He played with his half-empty wine glass, avoiding her gaze. 'Water under the bridge.'

Looking at him, Foxie thought he was probably more upset than he cared to admit. Hopefully, it was only his pride that was hurt.

He glanced at his watch. 'And it's getting late. Much too late to start talking business now.'

'Oh Daniel! And that was the reason I stayed — '

'Was it?' He gave her a direct look, raising his eyebrows. 'You said you were staying in town to buy clothes?'

'Yes, but I wanted to thrash all this out without Mum around.'

To her surprise, he laughed. 'Your mother? She'd run a mile before letting herself be drawn into a business discussion of any kind.'

Foxie thought about it for a moment and nodded. 'I suppose you're right.'

'Look, anything we discuss now will be beer talk — theory at best. I'll get some figures together and bring them down to show you in a day or so.'

'You could have arranged all that with me this morning and let me go home.'

'Still feeling vaguely suspicious and resentful? Come on, Foxie, be honest.'

'I suppose so, yes.' She avoided his penetrating gaze.

'And surely this is more fun? I've had a great time this evening and — forgive me — but until a few moments ago, I thought you did too.'

'Of course I have. We've had a lovely meal and it's been great but I really shouldn't — '

'Shouldn't what? It's always the same with you, isn't it, Foxie? I've never known such a woman for creating difficulties where there are none.'

'Now that isn't fair.'

'Perhaps we should reconsider this partnership, after all. It could be a big mistake.'

'My thoughts entirely.' She lifted her chin, steadily meeting his gaze.

Suddenly, he was all efficiency, signalling to their waiter. 'So, if there's nothing else you would like? Coffee, maybe?'

'Thank you, no.' She placed her napkin on the table beside her plate, indicating that she was ready to leave.

'Then I'll settle the account.'

If the limousine driver was aware of the frosty atmosphere between his passengers, who were gazing out of separate windows and ignoring each other, he knew better than to show it. He drove them smoothly and sedately to Daniel's house and sprang out to open the door for Foxie, handing her out of the car as if she were royalty.

'I have it!' Suddenly, he gave up all pretence of formality. 'I know who you are. Carole Parker from *The Brave and the Free*! My wife will never forgive me if I don't get your autograph — and, if you don't mind, a photograph on my cell phone.'

Dutifully, Foxie asked for his wife's name and wrote a greeting on the back of the card he presented. Then she posed for the photograph with her best 'Carole Parker' sneer. Daniel watched all this, waiting somewhat impatiently, at the front door. Photo opportunity over, the driver was happy to leave and Foxie looked up at Daniel, standing at the top of the steps.

'I don't think I'll stay the night, after all,' she called up to him. 'Lot to do in the morning. I'd rather get on home.'

He was down the steps and beside her in an instant. 'Foxie, you can't. You might think you're OK, but we've shared more than one bottle of good wine tonight and it's potent stuff. Where will you be if you lose your licence for being over the limit?'

'I won't lose my licence. I'm quite sober and I'd very much rather go home.'

'No way. What if you fall asleep and drive into a truck?' Before she realized what he would do, he plucked her little gold evening purse from her hand and bounded back up the steps to the front door.

'How do you know I don't have my keys in my pocket?' she tried. He shook the purse and grinned when he heard the satisfying jingle of keys inside.

'Daniel! Don't be an idiot. Just give me my purse.'

'You'll be the idiot if you try to drive tonight. Sleep in the bed Mrs Wicks has made up for you and she'll make you breakfast when she gets in about nine. You won't even have to see me, if you don't want to. I'll be in the office by eight.' He unlocked the front door, ushering her inside.

'You're such a bully.' She scowled.

'I know, but this time it's for your own good.'

'I hate it when people say that.'

'Oh, so do I.' He didn't seem in the least concerned. 'Now, if you don't mind, Foxie, I'll show you to your room and leave you to it. You'll find a bathroom *en suite*. Toothbrushes and soap in the vanity.'

'My purse?' She held out her hand for it.

'Not yet. I don't want you sneaking out in the middle of the night. I'll leave it on the hall table in the morning.'

Fuming, she had no option but to follow him up what must once have been the back stairs, leading to servants' quarters. The walls of the small, austere servants' bedrooms had been removed to make one large room containing a huge king-sized bed. Beyond, she could just see an adjoining bathroom decorated in green and black marble, a modern art deco style. She hadn't experienced such luxury since she went on location to Italy with *The Brave and the Free*. There was even an electric jug on a side table, complete with a tray containing several packets of tea, coffee and milk, in case she needed a drink before going to bed. Daniel's Mrs Wicks had thought of everything.

'I'm sure you'll be comfortable,' he said formally, as if he were the concierge rather than her host, satisfied to see that for once she had nothing to say, completely in awe of his renovations. With that, he nodded, turned on his heel and walked out, closing the door softly behind him.

Left to herself, Foxie felt suddenly bleak. How had it happened? She had managed to quarrel with Daniel over nothing at all. He had planned a celebration which ought to have been a memorable evening for both of them, but she had ruined it; in the first place by quizzing him about Suzette and then by making him doubt the wisdom of taking her into partnership. She had been taking too much for granted. Far too much. If Daniel changed his mind about everything now, where would that leave her mother?

Too tense to sleep immediately, she decided to have a bath. There was a jar containing rose-scented bath salts and she scattered a generous handful into the water before getting in. Idly, she wondered who might have left them there. Daniel's French girl, perhaps? No, she wouldn't go there; she wasn't going to let her imagination work overtime on Suzette. Allowing the water to cover the whole of her body up to her chin, she sighed and lay back in the steamy, relaxing atmosphere, reminding herself not to fall asleep. It wouldn't do for Daniel's housekeeper to find a drowned woman in the bath in the morning.

Fifteen minutes later, her tensions had

dissolved and she was pleasantly tired, ready for bed. She dried herself on the fluffy, white towels left ready on a warm towel-rail and examined her face, bare of the heavy make-up she had worn to go with her glamorous coat. Without it, she looked very young indeed, her features still unlined.

Having no nightgown she slipped into bed naked, enjoying the feel of cream satin sheets under the warm winter duvet. Books were provided on the bedside table, hot off the best sellers' lists, but she was in no mood to read. She turned off all the lights and snuggled into the pillows, composing herself for sleep.

She was almost there when her eyes snapped open again and she was immediately wide awake, heart thudding. Had she really heard it or was it the start of a bad dream? The sound came again and she whimpered, recognizing it all too well. Although she strained to see in the darkness, she could hear rather than see the creature scampering upside down across the ceiling.

She lay there frozen for a moment, screwing up the courage to put on the bedside light. No further sound came and she breathed more easily, ready to be convinced it was a nightmare, after all.

In these unfamiliar circumstances, it took her a moment or two to find the switch and she blinked as her eyes adjusted to the light flooding the room. Hardly daring to move her head, she raised her eyes to the ceiling and looked carefully in all four corners. There was nothing there. She almost laughed with relief.

Then it moved and she saw it. An enormous brown speackled spider, legs splayed, hanging by a thread of its own making, slowly descending towards the foot of the bed. Foxie's courage deserted her and she screamed.

★　★　★

After leaving Foxie, Daniel went to his own quarters, cursing himself for a fool. What a bear he was, always letting his temper run away with him. And why did it always happen around Foxie? It had been the same ever since they were infants together, as if she were the catalyst, the match always lighting his fuse and igniting a bomb.

He heard water running through the pipes and knew she must be taking a shower or bath. Good. It was a pity the evening had ended on a sour note but it pleased him to know she was making herself comfortable in his home. Tired and aware that he had a busy day ahead of him tomorrow, he lay spreadeagled in bed, composing himself for sleep. He was just reaching that first level of drowsiness when a woman's terrified scream brought him fully awake, curdling his blood.

It was Foxie who had screamed! Was she being attacked? Was there a burglar in the house? Pausing only to pull on his robe and grab the baseball bat he kept in a bedside cupboard for just such a purpose, he bolted along the corridors to the other side of the house. She heard him arrive and called out in an urgent whisper.

'Daniel, be careful. Don't make any sudden moves.'

Cautiously, he pushed open the door, half expecting to see Foxie held hostage by an intruder brandishing a knife or a gun.

She was sitting at the top of the bed, hugging the pillows, her knees drawn up to make herself small as possible. He followed the direction of her horrified gaze to see a large female huntsman marching purposefully across the duvet at the bottom of the bed. He wanted to laugh with relief but knew this wouldn't endear him to Foxie. Instead he said, 'Oh, that's rather a healthy specimen, isn't it? Better not clout it, then. It'll make a mess of the duvet.'

'Daniel, I don't care how you dispose of it but do something quickly, please. If it comes anywhere near me, I swear I'll — '

'OK. OK. Keep your hair on.' He signalled for her to be quiet, whistling softly, almost under his breath.

'What are you doing?' she said in agonized tones. 'Spider whispering?'

He shook his head, continuing to whistle softly until a beautiful Siamese cat came into the room, lashing her tail and answering him in her loud, Siamese voice.

'Oh no,' Foxie groaned in despair. 'Don't leave it to Lady Thiang. She's so cross-eyed, she can see two of everything. Even if she catches it, she'll lose it again.'

'Ssh! Don't say that, you'll offend her.' Daniel frowned in mock seriousness. Gently, he lifted the cat on to the bed and her eyes widened with feline glee as she assessed the size of the intruder. Lady Thiang was swift and efficient, pouncing on the spider and piercing it with her sharp claws before catching it up in her mouth and running away as if she were afraid of being robbed of her prize.

'Ugh,' Foxie shuddered. 'Will she be all right with that? It won't poison her?'

'Not she. I'm afraid she finds them a delicacy. She catches a spider most days. This is an old house.'

'Haven't you thought of calling a pest exterminator?'

'And spoil the cat's fun?'

Foxie managed a wobbly smile. 'Daniel, I'm sorry but I can't sleep here now. Not under that duvet. I'll just imagine that creature walking over it all night.' Gingerly, still shivering, she wrapped one of the sheets around her like a toga and got out of bed.

'Well,' he thought for a moment. 'I suppose you could have my room and I'll sleep here — '

'No, no you don't understand. I'll have nightmares. I always do when I've seen one of those.'

'Foxie, you need to get help for this phobia. You can't let it rule your life.'

'I know,' she said through gritted teeth. 'But there's not much I can do about it at this time of night. Can't I sleep in your bed?'

He narrowed his eyes at her. 'Now let me get this straight. You're saying you want to sleep in my bed? With me in it?'

'Yes, please.'

'Phew.' He blew out a long breath. 'I dunno. That's asking for a lot of self-control from a red-blooded male.'

'Put a bolster down the middle of it, if you like. I promise you, it's the only way I'll get any sleep tonight.'

'Well, I doubt if I will,' Daniel grumbled, but, seeing Foxie was gathering up her clothes, determined to spend not a moment longer in his spare room, he gave in and led the way back to his own room.

Seeing his bedroom again brought back to Foxie all the better memories of their old love affair. It seemed little altered from the time she had shared it with him before. His dressing chest stood in the same place and he still kept that wonderful picture of the wild horses of the Carmargue hanging on the wall opposite the bed. More than once, she had tried to wheedle him into giving it to her but he never would, promising only to keep it for her instead.

'Oh!' she breathed, catching sight of it. 'You still have my picture.'

'*My* picture,' he corrected, busying himself with a pile of spare pillows to mark the centre of the bed. 'I like to keep familiar things around me. They make me feel secure.'

Foxie glanced at him for a moment, finding it hard to believe that someone like Daniel could ever feel insecure.

'There,' he said, patting the last pillow into place. 'Do you still like to sleep on the right hand side?'

She nodded, pleased that he should remember.

While she dropped the sheet and climbed into bed, unselfconsciously naked, Daniel found a pair of jockey shorts before parting company with his robe. Although outwardly he retained his composure, his body seemed to have ideas of its own, responding vigorously to the thought of Foxie sharing his bed even with a wall of pillows between them.

Foxie herself was just as disturbed. The bed smelled pleasantly of young, healthy male, overlaid with Daniel's trademark cologne, tantalizing her with memories she had thought crushed and buried forever, but which now returned in full force to torment her: Daniel's fingers tracing the length of her spine, making her shiver in anticipation of the fiercer lovemaking yet to come; Daniel's lips on her skin, at her breast, patiently teasing her until he sensed she was there with him, ready to open herself as a flower must open to the sun. No! Why did she have to think of that now, making her body tingle with a longing that wasn't about to be assuaged.

The truth was that she was lying here uninvited in Daniel's bed and, judging from the way he had so swiftly built the barrier of pillows between them, it was clear that she was unwelcome there. She was making a fool of herself in more ways than one. He was probably still in love with his French girl. The least she could do now was pretend to fall asleep, allowing them both to get some rest.

On the other side of the bed, Daniel was consumed with similar thoughts. What was she doing to him? Climbing naked into his bed and expecting him to take it in his stride and quietly go off to sleep. Did she think he was made of stone? Or was it some sort of test? Yes, that must be it. She was testing him to see whether or not they could maintain a platonic relationship. Well, if that's what she wanted, she would find out the measure of his self-control. He wouldn't let himself think of that gorgeous, high-breasted body lying on the opposite side of his bed, nor would he think of those wonderful, long, California-tanned legs or her beautiful, slender feet. He wasn't going to remember the special salty-sweet taste of her skin or the soft moan of surrender as her lips softened and parted under his own. Before he could stop himself, he groaned aloud.

'Daniel?' she whispered urgently in the darkness. 'Are you OK?'

'No, I am not OK,' he growled, sitting up and turning on the bedside light, starting to hurl the pillows that separated them out of the bed.

'What are you doing?' She tried to keep the exultant giggle out of her voice.

'I'm going to make love to you — '

'Daniel, wait! Don't you want to think

about it for a moment? Is this wise?'

'I don't care any more. I don't care if you think it's wise or not or if we're going to regret it tomorrow and for the rest of our lives. But I can't stand it a moment longer. I want you here in my arms, if only for this one night.'

It was the familiarity that undid her. The warmth of Daniel's body and the way he fixed her with that feral gaze before enfolding her in his embrace. Finally, she felt the whole length of his body against her own as well as the thrilling heat of his arousal. His kiss was familiar too, making it all the sweeter. It felt like coming home. He teased her lips with his tongue before deepening the kiss until he felt she was ready for him, her body tensing under his own.

Greedy for each other, they didn't wait, Daniel pausing only long enough to find a packet of condoms in the bedside table. Foxie blushed, hiding her face in her arm. She realized that if he hadn't thought of it, she would have abandoned herself to lovemaking without protection They came together urgently and noisily, almost fighting each other in their desire for closeness, working towards release. Foxie had her legs wrapped around his hips, head flung back and eyes fluttering, her hands clawing his shoulders until he caught her wrists and held them down to prevent her from drawing blood. She didn't seem to know her own strength; it was rather like having an untameable tigress in his bed. In a detached part of his mind it occurred to him that he might be the victim of her frustration. It must have been a very long time since Foxie last made love.

Just as suddenly, it was over and she stared at him wide-eyed, her bosom heaving as if she had run a marathon. In a sense, she had.

'I'm so sorry,' she whispered, still short of breath. 'I didn't hurt you did I?'

'Isn't that supposed to be my line?' he teased. 'It's OK. I know how to defend myself.'

She lay back, still breathing heavily, as he leaned over and gently kissed each of her breasts.

'You're so lovely,' he whispered, leaning on his elbows to look at her, his eyes warm with affection and satisfied desire. 'Four years have improved you; you're even lovelier than I remember.'

'Oh Daniel, don't talk,' she whispered, drawing his head towards her to kiss him again, her body still aching with need of him. This ignited the fire again although it didn't burn quite so fiercely as before as they clung together, exploring and savouring each other as they went through the familiar dance of love. It was a long time before they fell asleep in each other's arms.

Foxie didn't hear him leave, sleeping dreamlessly until she was woken by a knock at the door, aware that someone had come into the room without waiting for her to respond. The curtains were thrown back to let in a morning of bright sunshine and for a moment she was disoriented, unable to remember where she was. In a hotel bedroom? But she didn't remember ordering room-service. Then she realized that the motherly figure wearing an old-fashioned overall patterned with forget-me-nots was unlikely to be a staff member of any modern hotel. Only then did the events of the previous night come rushing back to her and she realized this had to be Daniel's Mrs Wicks.

'I left you asleep as long as I could, dear, but it's past ten o'clock.' The old lady smiled at her.

'Ten o'clock!' Foxie sat up so suddenly, the sheet fell away, revealing her nakedness. 'I should've been on my way ages ago. I'm so sorry,' she said introducing herself, 'you must be Mrs Wicks. I'm Jane Marlowe.'

'Oh, I know who you are, dear. Mr Morgan told me all about you. Although I had a bit o' trouble findin' you.' Knowing blue eyes twinkled at Foxie. 'He said you'd be in the spare room.'

'I'm afraid it's a long story.' Foxie smiled ruefully.

'That's all right. You don't have to explain yourself to me, dear. I'm quite used to Mr Morgan an' his ways.'

'Did he leave any message for me?'

'No, dear.' Mrs Wicks gave her a kindly look that Foxie hoped wasn't pity. 'But I'm sure he'll be in touch Now, you eat that breakfast before it gets cold. Nothing like scrambled eggs to set you up for the day. You'll find me downstairs if you need anything,' she said on her way to the door. 'I'll be here until twelve.'

'Thank you, Mrs Wicks,' Foxie said absently, still dwelling on what the woman had just said. She said she was used to Mr Morgan and his ways. What did that mean? That she was *used* to finding naked girls in his bed? Was she just another conquest, after all? And a pathetically easy one at that, having invited herself there. She went over everything that had happened once more in her mind. He had said she was lovely, yes, and she knew he wanted her but as what? She could recall no time during that long night when he said that he loved her, not even in the throes of passion.

And how should she behave when she saw him again? Would he expect her to be 'grown-up' about it and ignore what had happened last night? She realized now that the last four years had been a farce; she wasn't 'over' Daniel, not at all. If only that wretched spider hadn't come marching into her bedroom, she would have spent the night where she was supposed to be and it would have been business as usual today. Instead she was left with a dilemma of her own making.

Finding herself ravenous, she applied herself to Mrs Wicks's delicious breakfast. Fresh orange juice followed by filtered coffee, hot and strong just as she liked it, the lightest scrambled eggs she had ever tasted, followed by toast and a small pot of home-made marmalade. Daniel's Mrs Wicks was indeed a treasure. Did he ever lie in bed long enough to receive such treats? Or was it just his way of rewarding ladies who stayed the night? Now you stop that! She told herself sternly. You're reading too much into a casual remark and letting your imagination run away with you. But the casual remark had been made, unintentional as it might have been, and was now eroding Foxie's new-found happiness.

5

Daniel was as good as his word. The very next day he arrived at the Marlowe stables with so many plans and pages of figures, it made Foxie's head spin. But if Marion had secretly cherished the idea that their love affair might be rekindled, she was doomed to disappointment. Foxie had returned home looking tired and was close-lipped about the events of the previous night, more interested in showing her mother the clothes she had bought.

'Yes, dear, but these are just clothes.' Marion wasn't to be diverted. 'I want to hear about your night out. Where did Daniel take you?' Her eyes widened with pleasure when Foxie mentioned the famous and exclusive Chinese restaurant, but her smile soon gave way to concern when she heard of their visit from the woman who wasn't a fan.

'I hope she didn't spoil your evening.' Marion shivered. 'People like that can be strange; they can turn into stalkers. Maybe you should mention it to the police.'

'Whatever for? Besides, there's nothing to tell. I don't know anything about her except that her name is Stella.'

'Well, that's a start, isn't it? I still think you should take it more seriously.'

'No, Mum.' Foxie laughed. 'She's had her run in with Carole Parker and that's all she wanted. I don't expect to hear from her ever again.'

'Well, I hope you're right.' Marion sounded far from convinced.

But all thoughts of the deranged fan and the evening out were forgotten when Daniel arrived the next day with a briefcase filled with cash projections and proposals.

Alarmed at the prospect of being drawn into business discussions, Marion discovered an urgent need to visit the supermarket and took off just as Daniel said that she would.

Left alone with him, Foxie was wondering how to broach the subject of the night they had spent in each other's arms, or whether it might be best to leave well alone and say nothing at all. In the cold light of day, seeing Daniel dressed for business as usual, it was hard to imagine him as the man who had taken her to the heights of passion only the night before. The only evidence that remained was that he seemed just as cautious and ill at ease as she felt herself.

The awkwardness that existed between them was her own fault entirely for throwing herself at his head and she knew that if they were to stand any chance of moving on to a viable working relationship, she must find a way to let him off the hook.

'Um, about the other night.' She plunged straight in, deciding there was nothing to be gained from hesitation.

'Yes?' he responded eagerly, his gaze meeting her own, ready to hear what she had to say.

'Daniel, I'm sure you realize — as I do — that it was a mistake — '

'A mistake?' He wasn't helping, keeping his expression determinedly blank.

'Yes. It was an accident of fate — a one-off — a kind of laying of ghosts, you might say.'

'You might.' His smile faded and he sat back, folding his arms, regarding her.

'Daniel, stop repeating everything that I say. You're not making this any easier. I'm trying to apologize for throwing myself at your head.'

'What for? I had a great time. So did you,' he added flippantly. 'End of story. I'm sure we're both grown-up enough to see it in the right perspective.'

She felt as if he had just slapped her across the face. So it had meant nothing to him, absolutely nothing at all. If she said any more, she'd be making a fool of herself.

She took a long breath and expelled it. 'I'm

so relieved. It was over between us a long time ago, so as long as we understand each other,' she gave him her brightest smile.

'Everything's fine.' He finished the sentence for her.

She took a deep breath and changed the subject, glancing at her watch. 'Jim should have the horses back from their track work by now. I think we should take all this over to his office. I'd like him to sit in on our discussions.'

'Good idea. Jim may be a pessimist but he has a practical turn of mind and I value his input.'

At the stables, work was in full swing, feeding and grooming the horses after their exercise. A diminutive grey caught Foxie's attention and she leaned over the door to look at her. 'That's a nice little filly,' she remarked. 'I don't think I've seen her before.'

'Hopefully, the first of many,' Daniel joined her. 'Presently, Mighty Minnie belongs to me. Jim has been training her. If she can win her race against other fillies and mares in town at the weekend, she'll be the spearhead of our operation. There are already several interested parties who want to take shares.'

'She certainly looks the part.'

'Foxie likes our Minnie.' Daniel greeted Jim with this news as he came up to join them. 'What d'you think of her chances at Flemington on Saturday?'

'Fair.' Jim scratched his chin, never one to enthuse. 'Long as the rain holds off an' those silly beggars don't over-water the track. She ain't no mud runner.'

'We'll see, then.' Foxie led the way to Jim's office and waited while he cleared newspapers and jackets from the extra chairs.

'Sorry about all the mess.' He started gathering papers into a pile. 'If I'd known I was havin' visitors . . . '

'We're not visitors, Jim,' Daniel said as he occupied the seat behind the desk, 'and never apologize for a mess: it's the sign of a busy man. Only the idle have time to be tidy.'

Jim grinned. 'Never thought of it like that.'

It took over an hour for Daniel to show them all that he had in mind and at the end of it both Foxie and Jim were impressed.

'So how many horses do you think we need to get started?' she said. 'And what sort of investment are you likely to want from me?'

'That depends on whether we go for top bloodstock or punt on nobodies that seem to show a bit of promise.'

'Maybe we can have both.' Foxie smiled.

'If I were to do it all on my own, I could afford two more promising horses. And I think it will pay us to get the best on offer. If you put up some money as well, we can spend some of it on our promotion and probably get two more, making five in all. I think there should be a limit of six shares on each horse; we don't want too many amateurs swarming all over the place.'

'No, indeed.' Jim said. 'An' we should have set times for visitin' too — like the hospital.'

'But we're not a hospital, Jim. We must make our clients welcome and feel they're getting value for their money.'

Jim pulled a face.

'I know how you feel, Jim.' Foxie grinned. 'Everyone would love to run a business that didn't need customers. But I agree with you; there should be set times for us to entertain clients. Say, Sunday afternoons and maybe one other day in the week when we have no horses racing.'

'There won't be too many of those,' Jim grumbled, still unwilling to co-operate.

'These are just details.' Daniel started gathering his papers to bring an end to the fruitless discussion. 'I'm sure we can work something out. First we have to attract the clients. We can work out how to regiment them later on.' He glanced at his watch. 'Hey! Doesn't time fly when you're having fun. I must get back to town.'

'Oh?' Foxie shot him a quick glance. 'Mum

was hoping you'd stay and have dinner with us.'

'Not this time, thanks all the same.' He shrugged. 'Got to oversee the opening of a new fitness complex at seven o'clock. See you at Flemington on Saturday though. Mighty Minnie is going to need our support.'

'And I'll look over these figures and do some sums of my own. Then I'll let you know how much I can invest.'

'You are coming in, then?'

'Oh, I think so.' She smiled. 'It's a great idea. Obviously, I'll need to check out a few things but you do seem to have the Midas touch'

'So people tell me.' He nodded.

As Daniel drove away, nursing his car along the Marlowes' ill-kept drive, he congratulated himself on handling what could have been a difficult situation. He had shaken hands with Jim and not even tried to kiss Foxie goodbye. Just as he feared, she regretted everything that had happened between them the night before. It was his own fault entirely for rushing things. Badly frightened, she had come to him for protection and in response he had all but ravished her, giving her no time to consider her options. No wonder she was now saying it was a mistake. He had behaved like a selfish teenager and her present attitude was no more than he deserved. Well, he would respect her wishes and keep his distance. Until she indicated otherwise, it would be strictly business between them from now on.

★ ★ ★

Saturday morning dawned crisp and fresh, heralding one of those bright, unusually sunny days that Melbourne can turn on in winter. Jim set off early with Mighty Minnie and her stablegirl, Wendy, in the Marlowe float, accompanied by one of their older mares, Green Ginger, who was entered in the same race. Rose arrived at the house soon after breakfast and was now closeted with Marion, trying on hats. Half an hour later, Foxie decided to hurry them up.

'Come along you two, it's nearly half past nine already. We've got an hour's drive even before we get to the city and Flemington's on the other side of town.'

'I know very well where Flemington is, darling, but I can't decide between this blue straw or the navy felt cloche.' Her mother sighed.

'For goodness' sake, Mum, wear the cloche. The straw won't fare very well if it rains.'

'Oh, do you think it'll rain?' Marion glanced at the light-weight suit she was wearing. 'Perhaps I should wear the brown wool after all. But then I'll have to find another hat.'

'Marion, come along.' Rose plonked the cloche firmly on her friend's head. 'You're driving your daughter mad.'

But Marion wasn't listening, having just noticed that Foxie was dressed in an old grey suit with a pleated skirt, no jewellery or even a hat.

'Why on earth are you wearing that old thing? It's been in the cupboard for years. You didn't even bother to take it to America.'

'Mum, it'll do. This isn't a major race day and I want a chance to be an observer without drawing too much attention to myself. Now let's go, please, or we're going to miss the whole day.'

Marion allowed herself to be hustled out of the house, still grumbling about her daughter's appearance.

'Nobody cares about looking well turned-out any more. Before we know it, they'll be letting people wear jeans in the members' enclosure. Girls will be getting married in them next.'

'They already are,' Foxie said as she settled the two women into the car. 'In Las Vegas I saw a couple — '

'I don't wish to know,' Marion sniffed. 'Standards are slipping everywhere.'

On arrival at the track some two hours later, they found Daniel had arrived before them and was already looking over the horses as they stood in their allotted stalls, awaiting the race. Today he had brought his secretary along, neatly turned-out in a dark green suit, trimmed with cherry red velvet and wearing a jaunty red velvet cap to match.

'Who's that girl with Daniel?' Marion said in a stage whisper, earning herself a dig in the ribs from Foxie.

'Be quiet, Mum. It's just Daniel's PA,' she murmured, despairing of Marion's tactlessness.

'Too pretty by far. And she should be wearing the grey suit, not you.' Marion wasn't to be silenced so easily. 'And you know what they say — red hat: no knickers.'

'Give the kid a break, Mum. She's not old enough to know that one.'

'Well, it probably still holds true.'

At this point Daniel joined them and entered the conversation. 'I asked Pepper to come along to take note of any enquiries and get details from interested parties. She'll be looking after the paperwork so I want her to have a good grasp of everything.'

'Isn't it exciting?' Pepper enthused, enjoying the spectacle of the horses parading in the ring. 'I've never been to the races before. I don't even know how to bet.'

'I'll help you, but I'm sure you'll soon learn,' Rose said kindly. 'Most people have beginner's luck.'

'She won't,' Marion chimed in. 'Not wearing green. Don't you know it's unlucky to wear green to the races?'

'Is it?' Pepper looked crestfallen.

'Nonsense, Marion.' Rose was brisk. 'Where do you find all these awful old sayings?' She smiled at the little secretary who had come ready for action, clipboard in hand. 'Pepper and I are old friends — on the telephone, anyway. You know, there's something I've always wondered and never liked to ask. Why does Daniel call you Pepper? Is it your surname or just a nickname.'

'A nickname, really.' The girl sighed briefly, weary of explaining about her name. 'Don't laugh, but I was christened Persephone. Kids couldn't handle it so we shortened it to Pepper or Pep.'

'Persephone? Oh, you poor thing,' Rose stifled a giggle. 'Fancy saddling a child with a name like that.'

While this exchange was taking place, Daniel had drawn Foxie to one side. 'What were you thinking?' he said, pulling a face at the schoolmarmish grey suit. 'I expected you to be dressed to the nines. We need to make a good impression today.'

'I didn't want everyone going nuts about Carole Parker. I thought I'd keep a low profile so that people would think of the stables, not me.'

'But you're one of our selling points.'

'That's OK. If they're sharp-eyed enough, they'll spot the Gucci handbag and shoes.'

'Point taken.' He shrugged, still not entirely happy.

When the time came for Mighty Minnie's race, Jim, Daniel and Foxie went down to the mounting yard to speak to the jockey and give him last-minute instructions. Jim had chosen a promising apprentice to ride her, making use of the boy's two-kilo weight claim but now that the big day was here, Simon Grant seemed to be suffering from an attack of nerves, blinking and tapping his whip against his leg. Daniel and Foxie exchanged uneasy glances.

'You can wave the whip, if you like, but don't use it,' Jim warned. 'She's willing enough but if you hurt her, she'll throw you — she's done it before.'

The boy nodded, accepting Jim's instructions and comments, some of his confidence returning as he sprang into the saddle and started urging the filly out on the track. They watched him ride past the few late blooming Flemington roses, making a brave splash of colour against the dull wintry sky. Having flowered constantly since the spring, the second autumn flush was only now slowing down. Soon they would be pruned, ready to burst forth in all their glory again for the Melbourne Cup and the Spring Racing Carnival.

'Hope I did right there,' Jim was saying, almost to himself as he watched Simon urge Minnie into a canter as he took her out on to the track. 'I was torn. Didn't know whether to get an experienced man or take the boy with his claim.'

'Too late for second thoughts now, Jim.' Daniel was also watching Simon's progress as he urged the filly into a canter on the way to the starting gates. 'She looks well and you know you've done the best you can.'

The race was short and dominated by Minnie. Simon didn't go out in front, but stayed on the pace, just behind the two leading horses. In the straight, he asked the filly for speed and she responded, but still wasn't making up enough ground to catch them.

'No lad, no.' Jim was almost praying as he

saw Simon raise his whip.

And then he fumbled and dropped it. After losing his whip, no other option was open to him but hands and heels. Feeling the confidence of his touch, the filly went into overdrive, pounding past the leading horses and winning the race with a length to spare.

The stands erupted with shrieks from Rose and Marion who almost lost their hats in their excitement. Pepper also squealed and said she'd just made fifty dollars while Jim stayed cool, nodding his satisfaction and getting ready to praise the nervous apprentice.

Without thinking, Daniel pulled Foxie into his arms and kissed her soundly on the lips until her open, surprised eyes made him stop and let go of her so quickly she almost staggered. Her heart was thudding so hard she thought everyone must hear it and she could feel her cheeks aflame. Why did he have to have this effect on her when she knew it meant nothing to him? It was just a boil-over of his enthusiasm and delight in Mighty Minnie's win. The other horse from the Marlowe stables, Green Ginger, had managed to snatch fourth place, so everyone was well pleased with the day's result. Even Jim was smiling for once.

While Jim and the grooms went to load the

horses into the float for the journey home, Daniel and Pepper exchanged business cards with prospective clients and fielded enquiries generally.

Foxie looked around for her mother and Rose and saw they were both at the bar, sharing a bottle of expensive champagne. She wasn't so pleased to see that they had engaged the attention of half a dozen reporters. Marion was ingenuous, especially when she was celebrating, and never saw any reason to be discreet.

'Have a glass of bubbly, Foxie, and get rid of that glum expression.' She called to her daughter who saw she was well on the way to being merry. 'Anyone would think that we'd lost.'

'No thanks, Mum. I've got to drive.' She glanced at her watch. 'And we should get going.'

'Now?' Marion sounded plaintive as a child. 'But we're having such a good time and I've only just met these people. They want to know all about us.' She nodded towards the reporters also at the bar.

'Mrs Marlowe, call me.' A sharp-featured woman pressed a card into Marion's hand. 'I'd like to have a good long chat — hear what it's like being Carole Parker's mum. I'll bring a cameraman, too. You'll be paid, of course.'

'Paid for what, Mum?' Over the noise at the bar, Foxie had caught only the last few words.

'Nothing at all, dear.' Marion opened eyes wide with innocence. 'They want a little of our history that's all. Bit of publicity for the stables.'

Foxie narrowed her eyes and watched the hatchet-faced woman leave. She looked familiar but, as yet, she was unable to place her. She looked sharp and incisive, not the type to concern herself with a bit of publicity for the stables. It was another half hour before she could persuade her mother and Rose, who were still in party mood, to leave the racecourse. As they did so, she saw Daniel leaving with Pepper. The girl was smiling up at him with adoring eyes and Daniel had his hand protectively on her back. Seeing them so in tune with each other gave Foxie an unpleasant jolt. It was only then that she realized he had left without even bothering to say goodbye.

On the way home, she had plenty of time for introspective thought while Rose and Marion sat together on the back seat, counting their winnings and giggling like teenagers, which made her feel left out of things and oddly depressed. Of course, they had been drinking champagne and she hadn't but that wasn't enough to account for the sudden downturn in her mood.

What was she doing back home, after all? Who needed her really? Now that Jo had been despatched, her mother seemed perfectly happy in Rose's company and didn't seem to need her at all. She had turned her back on a lucrative career in LA and for what? Daniel and Jim had effectively taken over her father's business and they didn't need her either except for the money they hoped she would invest.

On the following Monday, she took Daniel's facts and figures to her solicitor, Harvey Watson. He had been a friend of the family for as long as she could remember and was now a spry sixty-something, still very alert and snapping his fingers at the thought of retirement.

After they had exchanged the pleasantries and settled down to drink coffee, he was silent, spending some time poring over Daniel's figures. Finally, he sat back with a sigh and took off his spectacles, pinching the bridge of his nose.

'Not that bad, Harvey, surely?' she joked.

'It's all very smooth and up to a point it makes perfect sense,' he said at last. 'But the business was supposed to be left to you. That was always your father's intention. I don't see why you need to pour still more money into a business that should have been rightfully yours.'

'That's exactly what I thought, at first. But my father left a financial disaster and the stables were in trouble. If Mr Morgan hadn't come to the rescue, Boulter Brothers would have taken us over and swallowed us up by now.'

'And who told you that? Mr Morgan himself, I suppose?'

'Well, yes,' Foxie said in a small voice. 'Look, Harvey, are you saying that Daniel Morgan isn't to be trusted? I've known him all my life. He's the son of my mother's best friend.'

'When you've been in business as long as I have, dear girl, you'll have seen it all. A son will cheat his own mother out of her life savings if his need is sufficient.'

'I'm sure Daniel wouldn't do anything like that.'

'Are you?' He studied her pensively before he spoke. 'Jane, you must be — what — nearly thirty now?'

'Twenty eight.' She wriggled uncomfortably in her seat, unsure what he was driving at.

'And you've spent ten years in America, gathering this little bit of security around you?'

'It's not all that little. And I won't need to spend it all.'

'Even so, I'd rather you didn't throw it away on a smooth, fly-by-night Johnnie-come-lately just because he can put a few figures together and make them look good.'

'So you're not happy? You don't like the idea?'

'The syndication plan, yes. I see how it could work. More investment from you, no.'

Foxie stood up, shaken by Harvey Watson's advice. She had expected him to be enthusiastic about the scheme. It was a shock to find out he wasn't.

'Of course, if you want to go ahead anyway, that's up to you. But don't just hand over money without being very certain where it's to be spent.'

She gave Harvey an absent-minded kiss on the cheek and let him show her out. He had given her much to think about.

Outside, she decided it was only fair that Daniel should know of her solicitor's misgivings and, as she was in the city already, it was a small matter to drop by his office.

Pepper's greeting was polite but wary and she made it clear that she didn't like people arriving without an appointment, not even if they were business associates or friends. But Daniel himself seemed delighted to see her

113

and ushered her into his office, warning Pepper to hold all calls and cancel an appointment he was scheduled to keep in one hour.

Choosing her words economically and mentioning nothing of 'smooth, fly-by-night Johnnies', Foxie told him of her solicitor's doubts.

'Solicitors are always cautious, it's their job.' He started to interrupt.

'Daniel, let me finish. He didn't say I shouldn't invest, just that I should be careful, that's all. And make sure I knew how my money was to be spent.'

'That sounds reasonable. I can't blame him for looking after your interests. OK.' He sat back in his chair. 'I won't take any money from you at all. You can spend it in New Zealand yourself.'

'In New Zealand?'

'There's a dispersal sale on the North Island next month. It's all arranged. I've already got two tickets for Auckland and a booking at one of their top hotels. Separate rooms, of course,' he added hastily.

'But how did you know I'd . . . ?' Foxie began, only to be interrupted by a red-faced and tearful Pepper bursting into the room.

'Daniel, how could you,' she cried. 'You were taking *me* to New Zealand.'

'Pepper.' He fixed her with a stern look. 'I've told you before about listening in on the intercom.' He softened a little. 'And I know what I said. But it makes more sense for Foxie to go; she understands horses. Her eye must be nearly as good as mine. Look, I'll make it up to you. The trip to New Zealand is going to be all about work, anyway. I'll treat you to a week in Port Douglas instead.'

Pepper's lips still quivered and she sniffed loudly, like a disappointed child. 'I don't want to go to Port Douglas all by myself. I was looking forward to going to New Zealand with you.'

Foxie said nothing but raised her eyebrows and for the first time Daniel realized that his youthful personal assistant, whom he took so much for granted, might entertain inappropriate feelings for him.

'Well,' Foxie said, breaking the awkward silence. 'If you did promise her, Daniel — '

'I haven't promised anyone anything,' he insisted, his temper rising. 'It is a business trip. As for you, Pep, you can have a week in either Port Douglas or the Gold Coast when I come back. You choose.'

'I'll take the Gold Coast, then,' Pepper said with a final sniff, knowing better than to turn her back on a good thing when she saw it. 'More night life.'

After that there was only Marion to consider and Rose was only too happy to leave her cottage, which could be cold and draughty in winter, and agree to move into the Marlowes' solid brick home with its roaring, open fire in the lounge and comforting Aga in the kitchen. It took no more than a couple of phone calls to make these arrangements and Foxie drove home again with plenty to think about. Although she had remained outwardly calm and unaffected, inwardly she was just as excited as Pepper at the thought of taking a week-long trip to New Zealand with Daniel. All the same, she reminded herself, there would be no repetition of the night she had spent with him in his home near the city. She had no intention of being caught by his fatal charm yet again.

As she slowed to enter the uneven driveway leading to home, she had to give way to a jaunty red sports car on its way out. At the wheel she recognized the hatchet-faced woman reporter from the races. She wiggled her fingers and stretched her lips into a smile as Foxie allowed her to pass. At that same instant, Foxie remembered who she was; the name just popped into her mind. Clare Mallis. And she was far from being an ordinary reporter. She had a regular column

116

providing amusing but spiteful articles to one of the Sunday papers. What could she possibly want with Marion Marlowe? Foxie swore under her breath. No good would come of it and certainly it could have nothing to do with publicity for the stables. And her mother must have deliberately arranged to see her today, knowing that she, Foxie, had an appointment with Harvey Watson in town.

'Clare Mallis. What did she want?' she tackled her mother, who was still seated at the tea table with empty coffee cups all around her.

'Good heavens — you *are* in a mood. I haven't seen you with a face like that since you were five years old.'

'Mum, listen to me. It's important.'

'D'you want a coffee? I think there's one left in the pot — or I'll make a fresh one.' She stood up ready to go to the kitchen.

'Mum, I don't want any coffee.' Foxie reined in her temper, remembering her mother's bereavement. 'I just want you to tell me what you said to that woman.'

'She was very nice. So sympathetic and kind about your dad.'

'Softening you up,' Foxie said under her breath.

'And she brought me those flowers. Singapore orchids. They don't smell of much but they're awfully pretty.'

'Never mind about the flowers, Mum. What did you talk about?'

'I don't remember, really. A man took some photographs and we chatted about this and that. Then she said it was great, that she had all she wanted and left.'

And no matter how she approached it, this was all Foxie could get her mother to say.

6

Daniel had a hire car waiting for them when they reached Wellington, that city greeting them in typical winter fashion with an enthusiastic blast of cold wind. Foxie shivered, glad of her warm jumper and short raincoat which kept out most of the draught. She was even grateful for the long, knitted woollen scarf that Marion had insisted on sending with her.

On the flight, as they descended towards the coast of New Zealand, which indeed looked as if it had been pushed up out of the ocean by a giant hand, Daniel pointed out several landmarks and brought her up to date with his plans to make the best use of their visit. Over the next few days they would take a leisurely cross-country drive to Auckland, pausing to make contact with breeders and look at any promising 2-year-olds on offer along the way. But his main objective was a special dispersal sale to be held in Auckland in five days' time, the owner being an elderly man who was retiring and had no family willing to take over his business. Already, Daniel had been warned that this was top quality bloodstock and there would be little likelihood of a bargain.

'Every sale has a bargain,' he told Foxie confidently. 'But this time I just want to get the feel of the place. I've always bought in Ireland or Europe before, but if I like what I see, I'll come over again for the yearling sales after Christmas.'

Alone with Daniel, away from the over-interested eyes of her mother and Rose, to say nothing of Pepper, Foxie discovered she could relax. They had always enjoyed each other's company, never at a loss for something to say, and she had forgotten how easily he could make her laugh. Although he was raised as a city dweller, Daniel had as great a love of the wide open spaces as she did and relished the freedom and fresh air of open countryside and the simple pleasures on offer there.

Having only a small population, New Zealand was delightfully unspoilt; it was like stepping back into an earlier age. The fields were green and lush, the hills, if not all that high, were undulating and green and the trees had been left to grow as tall as they wished; a paradise of woodland and open country. No surprise then that it should be chosen as a background for Tolkien's well-loved story of Middle Earth. It was England as people wished it could still be; a world full of forests, wild flowers and meadows, reminiscent of times long past. She sat back and sighed with contentment, enjoying the rolling open countryside and the oddly sharp peaks to some of the hills, a constant reminder of the instability that still rumbled way beneath the earth. Daniel seemed to read her thoughts.

'Of course, there's a price to be paid for all this,' he reminded her. 'The whole country is subject to earthquake. It's sitting on two tectonic plates. One day they could shift and it will all disappear again, taken back into the sea.'

'But not today.' She smiled at him. 'Not when I'm only just learning to love it so much. God wouldn't be so cruel.'

'You'd be surprised,' he said in a sombre tone.

They had an excellent lunch of fish and chips that they ate on their laps in the car, as they had arranged to call at a property and see some horses at two.

Since Daniel had made the appointment, Foxie hung back and let him do all the talking while she observed the father and son who hoped for their custom. It didn't take her long to decide that she didn't like or trust them at all. The father kept rubbing his hands together as if he could already feel their money against his palms and the son kept a fixed grin on his face, smiling even when he was talking. She wanted to catch Daniel's eye to give him the signal to make their excuses and leave but he seemed determined to stay and see what was on offer. So she allowed herself to be ushered outside to watch the first horse go through its paces.

'This one's custom-made for your purpose. Perfect.' The son nodded, smiling and somewhat breathless after running with the horse to show him off. 'Still a young 'un — go at least three years in a syndicate, no sweat.'

'Just a minute here.' Foxie was quick to pick him up. 'I thought you were showing us two-year-olds? So why do you say he's *still* a young horse?'

'Ah well, maybe he is nearer three — '

'And the rest,' Daniel put in. 'He looks at least four to me.'

'Still got his winter coat, hasn't he?' The lad was determined to brazen it out. 'Makes him look shaggy an' old.'

'Because he is shaggy and old.' Foxie turned towards the car. 'Come on, Daniel. These people are wasting our time.'

'Wait!' The older man hated prospective customers to leave without buying. 'We have others.' He turned on his son. 'Idiot. What were you thinking, showing the lady that?'

'I'm sorry,' Daniel said. 'But our time is short. We have other people and other horses to see.'

'Not pinning your hopes on that dispersal, are you?' The man stood in Daniel's path. 'You'll get nothing there. Anything good has been sold off already.'

'I'll take that chance.' Daniel sidestepped around him, following Foxie to the car.

As they drove off, leaving the disgruntled farmers behind, Foxie glanced across at Daniel and they both laughed.

'My father would have called them a right pair of shysters,' she said. 'Just how stupid do they think we are?'

'Not stupid — just new to the business. For a start, you look far too pretty to know anything about horseflesh. They expect a horsewoman to wear jodhpurs, smoke like a train and stride about the place like a man.'

Foxie laughed again, relishing the compliment. But it was getting late and they needed to find somewhere to stay the night. She said she would be just as happy with a modest bed and breakfast on the road, but Daniel had other plans. He wanted to drive to Napier to stay at a hotel that a friend recommended; a historic hotel which had started life in the early twentieth century.

'But Daniel, I didn't think we'd be staying anywhere posh,' she protested. 'I haven't brought anything other than jeans and some sweaters.' Too late she remember Marion's advice to pack at least one uncrushable dress.

'Then we'll have dinner in jeans and sweaters.' He shrugged. 'Or you can buy a skirt if you must. But I've been told not to miss this art deco hotel. Napier was once flattened by an earthquake and they rebuilt it again in the art deco style, exactly as it was. Tomorrow we can explore the local vineyards or there's a balloon flight if you fancy it?'

'No, thank you,' she said. 'I prefer to keep my feet firmly on the ground.'

When they arrived at Napier it was already dark and the hotel, lit up from outside, looked more imposing and grand than ever. Daniel drove the car straight into the hotel's car park, confident that their needs would be met.

'You're lucky, sir.' The receptionist smiled at him. 'We were fully booked but we've just had a cancellation — one of our best suites too with a view of the — '

'I'm sorry but we're not a couple,' Foxie broke in, hoping to forestall any embarrassment. 'I'll need a separate room.'

'Oh.' The girl bit her lip. 'I didn't realize. But the suite does have two separate bedrooms. There's a king-sized bed in the master bedroom attached to the sitting room and a separate smaller room with two singles. TV in both rooms and two bathrooms, of course. For a family, you see.'

'We'll take it — for tonight and tomorrow as well,' Daniel spoke up quickly and murmured to Foxie before she could make any further objections. 'You can have the main bedroom and I'll take the room with the singles.' Having said this, he turned to the receptionist yet again. 'And dinner tonight in your restaurant? Table for two?'

'Certainly.' The girl smiled, looking up at him through long eyelashes, clearly at a loss to understand why Foxie wasn't keen to share the king-sized bed with such a charismatic man.

While they were waiting to be shown up to their suite, Daniel sat down at the piano in the lobby and played a few experimental chords. When nobody came rushing out to ask him to stop, he surprised Foxie by playing a couple of Scott Joplin rags and earned himself a small round of applause from some other hotel guests who had stopped to listen.

Foxie waited until they had been shown up to their suite before mentioning something that had been weighing on her mind.

'It's one thing to share a suite with me,' she

125

said. 'We're business partners as well as old friends. But what if Pepper had been here with you instead?'

'Is that it?' He laughed. 'I knew something was eating you. I wouldn't have come here with Pepper — of course not.'

'Then why bring me?' she said softly. 'We're only here for a short time after all and it is rather out of our way.'

Ignoring the question, he glanced at his watch. 'Better freshen up and get down for dinner. They won't want to start serving us much after nine.'

Still not entirely at ease or certain of Daniel's motives, Foxie showered and put on the long black skirt she had bought in a hurry just before the shops closed. With it, she wore a figure-hugging, low-cut black sweater and in her cleavage a coral and mother-of-pearl pendant on a silver chain. Being one of the last things her father had given her, it was one of her favourite pieces of jewellery and she wore it often. Her hair had grown quickly and was almost down to her shoulders again. She brushed it into shining waves, the coppery tone accentuated by her unusual streak of white hair at the front. Quickly, she renewed her mascara, added a glistening lip gloss and a spray of her favourite perfume to be ready just as Daniel knocked on the door separating their two rooms.

He had changed from the clothes he had travelled in, although he was still casually dressed in a dark checked-shirt with buttoned-down pockets, and black chinos. His hair was still wet from the shower and he had combed it back so it seemed darker than usual, almost black, making his eyes look bigger, too. For a moment he stared at her, unsmiling.

'Will I do?' she said to break the sudden tension. He relaxed, smiled and held out a hand, ready to escort her to dinner. As she accepted it, Foxie's errant heart missed a beat. His hand was so warm and reassuring, clasping her own, that her good resolutions wavered; she no longer wanted to keep him at arm's length. Snap out of it! She ordered herself You mustn't do this. You can't let yourself fall in love with him all over again — you'll only get hurt. Remember what Mrs Wicks said: you mean no more to him than any other easy conquest. Although, now she thought about it, she couldn't remember precisely what it was that Mrs Wicks had said, only that it had grated on her at the time.

In the dining-room the lighting was subdued, the tables covered in starched white linen tablecloths and decorated with candles

127

surrounded by posies of sweet-smelling flowers. Expensive glassware shone beside each place. Old-fashioned silver gleamed on the sideboards, adding atmosphere, and light, inoffensive music played in the background, never intrusive enough to halt conversation. The napkins were also white linen and generous in size. Foxie had the feeling that she had been transported back to an earlier, much more elegant era.

'Cocktails first.' Daniel smiled at the wine waiter who appeared at the table as soon as they had been seated. 'I'd like a Martini, very dry, with an olive, and the lady will have . . . ' He raised an eyebrow at Foxie.

'Just mineral water, thanks. The sparkling kind.'

'You won't join me?' He looked disappointed.

'I need to keep my wits about me. Remember what happened last time we had dinner together?'

'That was the spider. Nothing to do with drink.'

Foxie shuddered. 'Don't even mention those things.'

'I'm sending you to a hypnotist when we get back to Aussie. A friend of mine swears by this old guy in Fitzroy — '

'Daniel, no. I'm not going to some old

crank who thinks the best way to cure my fear of spiders is to let the beastly things crawl all over me.'

'He's a hypnotist, Foxie, not a zoologist.'

'Fine. But can we drop the subject for now.' She buried her nose in the menu to hide from him. 'I don't want a cocktail but I would like some wine with my meal. White, of course, very dry.'

'Yes, ma'am.' Daniel pulled a little face and conferred with the waiter who recommended a Semillon.

Having spent the day out of doors, they were both famished, so conversation lapsed as they devoured a substantial meal of roast chicken and winter vegetables. After that, Daniel was still hungry enough to indulge himself with a large helping of apple and rhubarb crumble although Foxie declined, taking a small serving of ice cream instead. Coffee had been ordered and was sitting in front of them, along with a plate of chocolate mints.

'So,' Foxie said at last. 'Are you ready to answer my question, Daniel? Why did you bring me here?'

'I told you,' he said, deliberately misunderstanding her. 'Because you need to see how I'm spending your money. And besides, I value your expertise.'

'That's not what I meant and you know it.' Lazily she stirred the chocolate into her capuccino, unwilling to let him off the hook. 'Why did you bring me here? To this very special, old-fashioned, romantic hotel?'

'It is, isn't it?' He glanced around as if appreciating the ambience for the first time. 'I thought it would please you, that's all. You *do* like it, don't you?'

'Why wouldn't I like it? It's lovely.' She took a mouthful of coffee and scalded herself. 'But at the same time, I think I should make something clear.' She paused here, to be sure she had his full attention. 'I'm not going to sleep with you, Daniel. Not tonight or any other night on this tour.'

He didn't speak for a moment and she could see she had angered him. He pushed his coffee aside and pressed his lips together, controlling his temper with difficulty. When at last he looked up, meeting her gaze, she could almost see sparks flashing from his eyes.

'Just what exactly do you take me for? Do you think I've so little self-control that I'm going to jump on you the moment I get you alone up there? You've already made your feelings abundantly clear. You told me what happened between us was a mistake. Well, OK. I accept that. But it's no good pretending it never happened because it did.

We've been much more to each other than old friends and you can't blow hot and then cold and expect me to forget it.' Leaving his coffee untouched, he stood up, unable to sit opposite her any longer. 'I'm going to bed now and I suggest you do the same. We have a long day ahead of us tomorrow.'

'Daniel, please don't go — we need to talk about this.' His words stunned her; she had misread him completely.

But he was already striding away from her, pausing only to sign the docket offered to him by the waiter on the way out. She sipped her coffee and waited another ten minutes, hoping that when she got upstairs to their suite, Daniel would be safely in bed and asleep. She knew she had handled the situation clumsily but it wasn't in her nature to be other than direct.

Opening the door of the suite quietly so as not to disturb him, she found he had switched on the table lamps in the sitting-room and gone to his own room. The door connecting the two bedrooms was firmly closed. She could hear the television in his room broadcasting a chat show, canned laughter following each remark of the host. Occasionally, she could hear Daniel laughing too. It made her feel lonely and left out although she knew that was a dangerous emotion for her to be feeling right now.

Why was she being so cautious? So scared of being hurt? Would it really have mattered so much if she'd stolen another couple of nights with him in this wonderful place? Subconsciously, perhaps she had even hoped for it. Why else would she pack her designer collection of nightwear from LA instead of the sensible cotton nighties she wore at home? It wouldn't do to examine that question too closely. She smiled ruefully at herself. What an idiot she had been. By now she could have been sharing this opulent bed with Daniel instead of lying here, high on her dignity, miserable and alone. She even considered knocking on his door and trying to put things right between them but decided against it. Right now, he would still be angry and wouldn't believe a word she said. Tomorrow, when he was over his pique, she would try to mend matters between them.

Sleep didn't come easily. She lay awake, listening for sounds of movement next door but after a while there was no sound at all, not even from the television. She tossed and turned, sprawling across the bed until she was finally too exhausted to stay awake. Then she dreamed she was back in LA, playing Carole Parker again. She was standing in front of the cameras, but she couldn't remember her

132

lines. Cameron Carstairs was there too, tearing his hair and getting angry with her for wasting time. The soap ran on a tight budget and they couldn't afford too many takes. She awoke, burning with anxiety and relieved to find she had nothing more serious to worry about than Daniel sulking in the next room. A glance at the clock on the bed-head showed it was only half past three. Four hours at least until breakfast.

As she was awake anyway, she got up to go to the bathroom, scrubbing her fingers through her hair. It wasn't until she went to wash her hands that she saw that the basin was occupied — by a large brown spider. For a moment she froze, knowing she ought to turn on the tap and wash it away but unable to summon the courage to do so. What if it were to escape and run up her arm? Heart racing, she crept from the bathroom and closed the door quietly behind her. Could she leave it and hope it would be gone in the morning? No. She wouldn't be able to go into that room at all, knowing it might suddenly reappear. There was only one solution: she would have to wake Daniel.

She tied her flimsy silk dressing-gown around her, took a deep breath and knocked on the door connecting their two rooms. No answer. She knocked a little louder and there was still no reply. Cautiously, she opened the door and went in.

She put on the bedside light to find Daniel sprawled face down on one of the single beds, snoring gently. The room smelled agreeably of the warmth of his sleeping body but also faintly of booze. On the table beside him, she saw two small bottles of whisky from the mini bar, both empty.

'Daniel!' She reached out and touched his bare shoulder, shaking it gently. He smiled and murmured in his sleep but he didn't wake up so she shook it a little harder. 'Please wake up.'

'Wassamatter?' He sat up, blinking, still heavy with sleep. 'Is there a fire?'

'No,' she said in an agonized whisper. 'But there's a spider in my bathroom.'

His shoulders slumped. 'And you want me to deal with it? At this time of night?'

'Please.'

He laughed weakly. 'Foxie, you really will have to do something about this ridiculous phobia — '

'I know, I know.' She was almost dancing with impatience. 'But will you please deal with this one for me now.'

'Where is it?'

'In the basin. And you *will* get rid of it, won't you? My father used to lose them and pretend they were gone.'

Muttering something uncomplimentary under his breath, Daniel rolled off the bed, groaning. Having fallen asleep in his underpants, he was decent enough, but for warmth he pulled on the white towelling robe provided by the hotel.

He rolled up his sleeves and strode purposefully into the bathroom, Foxie hovering behind, wanting to make sure he vanquished the monster, but ready to run if it should evade him.

'I haven't seen one like this before,' he called back to her. 'It might be a rare species.'

'Daniel, I don't care if it's the last of its kind in the universe. Just get rid of it, please.'

'Yes, ma'am,' he said. 'Tossing him out of the window now. And I've put the plug in the sink so his mates can't come looking for him.'

'Thank you,' she said in a small voice.

He grinned. 'You know, Foxie, we really will have to stop meeting like this.'

'In the middle of the night — over spiders.' She returned his smile. 'Daniel, I'm so sorry about what I said over dinner. It was unjust and uncalled for.'

'No, it wasn't,' he said. 'I was angry only because you hit the nail so exactly on the head. I did bring you here in the hope of sweeping you off your feet. I had some crazy idea that away from home on our own, we might be able to recapture the mood and pick up where we left off.'

'Nothing can ever be quite the same as it was. But I can't blame you for expecting it — after the way I threw myself at your head. I blush to think of it now.'

'Well, don't. It'll clash with your hair,' He teased, trying to keep the mood light.

'And I know what most people think of actors. I've had to set them straight often enough. They think we're promiscuous and must have more interesting sex lives than anyone else. Most of the time, they couldn't be more wrong.' There was suddenly an unspoken agenda flying back and forth between them creating an awkward silence that made Daniel glance at his watch.

'Foxie, it's late — or early, however you look at it. We really should try to get some sleep.'

She caught his hand. 'Oh no, Daniel, don't go . . . '

'I think I should.' He released himself gently and backed off, stepping purposefully towards the adjoining room. 'The spider is long gone, I promise. You're perfectly safe.'

She ignored that remark and smiled as if she hadn't heard what he said. 'You didn't look at all comfortable lying in that single bed.' She patted the unused pillows invitingly. 'Wouldn't you rather share this one with me?'

'Not if I'm going to see a face full of regrets in the morning. You said you weren't going to sleep with me, remember? Not on this tour.'

'I changed my mind.' She held his gaze as she unfastened her dressing-gown to reveal the lacy, black American teddy she was wearing beneath. High cut so that it made her legs look longer than ever, it clung to her figure like a second skin, a garment created for the sole purpose of seduction. She was Carole Parker again and at her most dangerous.

'Don't do this to me, Foxie. Not unless you mean it.' He caught her by the wrists and sprang astride her, pressing her back against the pillows so that he could read the expression in her eyes. 'I don't like playing games.'

'This isn't a game, I promise,' she whispered, writhing in his grasp. Closing her eyes, she offered her lips with a long sigh. He resisted for just a few seconds, prolonging her anticipation and adding spice to the moment, before his lips descended on her own.

There was no doubt that Daniel was a good kisser. He never rushed in dripping saliva like a wild animal about to devour its prey. For a man so aggressively impatient in other areas of his life, as a lover he liked to take things slowly. He started by kissing her throat and then teasing her mouth with his lips, invading it only as he sensed the subtle changes in her mood.

He tasted of wholesome good health and the whisky he had been drinking and Foxie murmured her satisfaction as she relaxed into his kiss. All the same, she couldn't help wondering how many girls had come after her to fill the long gap of almost four years. While she had maintained a celibate existence, accepting only occasional dinner dates and allowing no one past her front door, she knew there had been at least one other girl in his life. And, although she didn't care to admit it, even to herself, there had been and maybe never would be anyone but Daniel in her own.

Once again, he starting kissing her throat and she knew he was leaving a bruise that would show tomorrow although right now she was too enraptured to care. He made a line of small kisses from her throat to her breasts, teasing them with his teeth through the silky black lace and making her groan with pleasure. Instinctively, she raised one leg against his hip, sensing his tension and alerting him to her readiness to make love. Totally absorbed in her now, he pushed the straps from her shoulders, his eyes lazy with passion as he prepared to make his final move.

'Daniel, wait,' she whispered urgently. 'Don't you have some protection?'

'A condom,' he groaned, falling away from her, the moment shattered. 'No, I don't. I'm afraid I took you at your word, I really didn't expect — '

'Hold the mood.' She sat up and searched in the drawer of the table beside the bed. 'Eureka!' She waved the little packet triumphantly aloft. 'I thought your fancy hotel wouldn't let us down.'

'You knew just where to look,' he accused, starting to scowl. 'You've done this sort of thing before.'

'Matter of fact I haven't, so don't start.' She glared back at him.

'Really? An innocent person doesn't wear sexy nightclothes.'

'Oh and what do you expect me to wear? Flannelette pyjamas? If you must know, I have a whole wardrobe of these and matching peignoirs.' She was being deliberately provocative now. 'They were a present.'

'From a man?' His scowl deepened.

'No. Although I should let you think so. From a sponsor of the show.'

'Ah.' He let go a long breath of relief and

relaxed, shaking his head. 'We really do have to stop this, Foxie.' Gently, he took her face in his hands, looking into her eyes. 'Being so prickly and jealous, tormenting each other with insecurities. It's too painful.'

'I know, I know. But you provoke me and my temper always gets the better of me.' She put her arms around his neck and leaned in to him. He kissed the top of her head and then turned her around to massage the tension from her shoulders until she closed her eyes and relaxed against him, almost purring like a cat.

'Oh Daniel, that's wonderful,' she murmured. 'You could have made a fortune as a masseur.'

'What makes you think I didn't?' he whispered into her ear, making her open her eyes in surprise and turn to lash out at him.

'Uh-uh.' He caught her wrists before she could do any damage and started kissing her in earnest; hungry, open-mouthed kisses which could only lead to one conclusion now. More than ready for him, Foxie moved to accommodate him and he thrust hard and strong, forcing a soft cry from her as they found their rhythm. This first time they were too eager for satisfaction, too deprived to wait and it was over too soon. Feeling as if they had fallen back to earth from the stars, they lay in each other's arms, drowning in each other's gaze and laughing softly until their breathing steadied and after a while, they were ready make love again.

'You are so amazing to me, so beautiful,' he whispered before falling asleep in her arms. She pushed his hair away from his eyes and watched him sleeping for a while, thinking how much younger he looked with the lines of tension smoothed away. Was it really possible that he loved her as much as she loved him? Those words had been scarce between them since they broke up four years ago, when in anger and bitterness he called her a selfish, ambitious woman and taken everything back. With that question still unanswered, she too fell asleep just around the time that they should have been getting up.

They slept until after eleven when the chambermaid came knocking at the door, expecting to clean their rooms. When she received no answer she let herself in. A cheerful Maori girl, she gave them a big smile and then hid it with her hand, embarrassed to find the couple still lying in bed.

'So sorry — I'll come back.'

'No, no, it's all right.' Foxie sat up and pulled her inadequate dressing gown around her and aware that the girl was looking at the darkening bruise on her throat. 'We're getting up now,' she said firmly, making Daniel groan and pull the covers up over his head. 'Yes, Daniel, we are.' She pulled them down again and turned to smile at the maid. 'You can start in the other room.'

7

They stayed another night in Napier, behaving like lovers on holiday, surprising each other with small gifts and visiting vineyards and generally enjoying themselves as tourists. On the following day they left Napier to resume the serious business of buying horses. But although they travelled all over the island, following up other leads, nothing quite measured up to their expectations. In the end, they had to pin all their hopes on the Auckland dispersal sale.

With two days to spare before the sale, Daniel suggested they spend one day exploring Rotorua and the other on a trip to the Bay of Islands to go snorkelling with dolphins. Foxie readily agreed, looking forward to meeting the creatures in the wild.

The weather was surprisingly good for the time of year and the dolphins, used to interacting with humans, splashed and played around them and when Foxie came out of the water, helped back on to the boat by the crew, she was laughing with joy.

'Did you see that?' she asked Daniel, who was already aboard. 'I actually touched a dolphin. It was swimming right alongside me. I had no idea they were so huge.'

'I'd forgotten what a good swimmer you are,' he said.

'My mother made sure of it after you almost drowned me. She booked me into a swimming class the very next week'

'You're never going to let me forget that, are you? You have a memory longer than an elephant. Good job you don't have a build to match.'

She took a swipe at him but he dodged it and dived neatly into the water, taking another swim before they were called back for the much anticipated barbecue lunch. The sea air had made everyone ravenous.

After the day out on the water, they drove to Rotorua where they marvelled at the muddy slurping of hot springs and actually lay in the warm waters of a river. Then the carefree part of their trip was suddenly over. They needed to drive back to Auckland to be on the spot and ready for the sale, due to commence the following day. Daniel said they would need to confer with the agent he had employed to provide them with a short list of likely horses. Also, he wanted time to examine them himself to make sure they were sound and that transport to Australia would be easy to arrange. They had to be sure of all these

144

facts before making any bid.

Foxie had been to sales with her father before but nothing quite on this scale. This complex was awesome in size and on the morning of the auction the car park was almost full, confirming the measure of interest in this particular sale. The horses were brought into a ring in the centre of the room, prospective buyers filling the stands on three sides in front of the auctioneer. Taking her hand and pulling her behind him, Daniel pushed his way through to some vacant seats at the front, determined both to see and be seen.

As they sat down, they felt the buzz of excitement about this particular sale and consulted the list the agent had provided, seeing that his suggestions were scattered throughout the day. Daniel had taken the time to examine all of them, crossing only one of the fillies off the list.

The bidding was fast and furious and Foxie was overwhelmed by the speed at which it seemed to climb thousands of dollars in a matter of seconds. As Daniel was more experienced and at home with the process, they agreed that he should do all their buying. It would be a sorry thing indeed to find out they had been raising the price against each other.

For the first hour or so, the bidding was keen and the prices too high. But as the day wore on and people started to drift away, discouraged by the lack of bargains or having purchased their needs already, gradually the prices began to steady into their range. They bought two promising bay fillies, ready to run, for just $20,000 each.

'Here he is,' Daniel whispered as a beautiful chestnut colt was led in. 'The one I told you about.' Foxie was so impressed with his gait that she couldn't take her eyes off him and, without speaking, pressed Daniel's hand: the signal they had agreed on for when she wanted him to bid. The colt had a loping, almost fluid stride, promising speed, and his coat shone with health and good grooming. He was so exactly what they wanted that Foxie groaned at the thought that they still might not be able to buy him. The bidding climbed quickly to $80,000 dollars and Foxie held her breath, thinking the colt was theirs. Then two more bidders came in quickly, pushing the price to a hundred thousand, making Daniel curse softly under his breath.

'Give it one more,' Foxie whispered. 'And if it goes higher than that, I'll be happy to let him go.'

They waited agonizing moments while the auctioneer called one hundred and ten thousand several times, still hoping for more, and it seemed an age before the hammer fell. Foxie gave a small scream and hugged Daniel as the colt was knocked down to them. Now they had three good horses to expand their new enterprise.

Later though, she had a twinge of buyer's remorse. 'I'm afraid I got carried away with the moment,' she said when they had settled their account and made arrangements for the horses to be transported to Australia. 'Maybe we shouldn't have spent so much on the colt. It was an emotional purchase and we could have bought four more horses at around twenty thousand and still had some change.'

'We followed our instincts and I don't think they'll let us down,' he said. 'The fillies are nice enough to race in the country but we do need to offer our clients the occasional city winner. And if he does well, when his racing days are done, we'll be able to sell him on to a breeder for a handsome profit.'

So she let Daniel pay for the fillies and agreed to pay the larger amount for the colt, to seal their bargain as partners and make a substantial contribution to the new enterprise. She knew Harvey Watson would scold her for taking such a large chunk out of her savings, but that couldn't be helped.

Pleased with their purchases and the

general success of their visit, Daniel no longer wanted to play the tourist and seemed anxious to get back to Melbourne, his thoughts turning towards his other business interests, neglected since he had been spending so much time on the Marlowe stables.

'Pepper's not too bad at managing on her own,' he said. 'But sometimes I forget she's only nineteen.'

'If there'd been anything urgent, Daniel, I'm sure she would have called you.'

'Not she.' He gave a wry smile. 'World War III could break out and Pep would try to handle it on her own.'

'Well, stop fretting, you'll find out soon enough.' Foxie grinned at him as they boarded the plane. It seemed to take longer to get to the airport and wait to be summoned aboard than the flight itself which took just under four hours.

While Daniel went to reclaim Lady Thiang from the upmarket kennels where she had been living a life of pampered luxury while he was away, Foxie collected her car from his space at the office and drove slowly home, mulling over the events of the past few days.

She had set out meaning to keep Daniel at a distance but it hadn't worked out that way, not at all. What had happened to all her good resolutions? She had no will power where he was concerned; he had only to look at her with that certain intensity to set her passions on fire. Even during the day, they had been so at ease in each other's company that, although no words had been spoken of love or commitment, she was almost certain he felt the same. Or did he?

As an only child who had been sent to a girl's school, she had grown up knowing very little about men except as creatures who inhabited her mother's kitchen and were interested in nothing but horses. Older now and more experienced in life, she knew they could see things quite differently. While Daniel had said that he didn't like to play games, what did he really mean? That he loved her and wanted her to take him seriously? Or merely that he didn't care to be aroused and left unrequited?

And while he had spoken freely of the business partnership that existed between them, she could recall no words of emotional commitment or love. He had said she was amazing, beautiful even, but those were the words any man would say to a girl he found in his bed. So, as she drove home, she felt as if clouds were gathering overhead and all the happiness of the past seven days leached away, allowing all her old insecurities and doubts to creep in.

★ ★ ★

Daniel didn't leave for the office until he had
left Lady Thiang back at home and settled
her in. Used to the routine of homecoming,
the cat ran all over the house to make sure
nothing had changed in her absence, before
springing into his favourite chair and folding
her paws, purring contentedly to find herself
in familiar surroundings once more. He
sighed, knowing his chair would be covered in
fine white hairs that would be almost
impossible to remove from his clothes, but he
hadn't the heart to move her.

As he walked into the office, Pepper
greeted him with a squeal of delight.

'Daniel, thank goodness you're back! I've
been so bored sitting here on my own.'

'Bored? You shouldn't be bored, you
must've been rushed off your feet.'

'Oh I was.' She waved a dismissive hand.
'But you know what I mean.'

'OK, shoot. What's been happening while I
was away?'

'Not a lot.' Pepper consulted her list to
remind herself. 'At the fitness centre a
woman fell down some stairs and she's
threatening to sue — '

'OK. Send that one round to the lawyers.'

'I already did. And we have at least ten

150

people clamouring to take shares in Mighty Minnie. I told them only six were available and you'd decide who could have them when you came home.' She turned up a file on her computer. 'There's a Mr Johnson, Mr Flood, Barry Glenn — you'd know him, he's on TV — a Mr and Mrs Patterson who like to be called Jim and Stella, and — '

'Whoa, Pepper. I'm sure it'll keep. Have you booked your holiday on the Gold Coast yet?'

The girl nodded eagerly. 'If it's all right with you, I'll take off next week.'

'Fine but make sure you get a temp in from the agency to cover your job while you're gone. Oh and this is for you.' He brought a small package out of his pocket.

Pepper gave another squeal and blushed to the roots of her blonde hair as she unwrapped a small jade tiki on a silver chain. 'Ooh Daniel, it's lovely. I'll put it on now.' She bent her head and held her hair out of the way as she waited for him to fasten it. He sensed her tension as he did so and it occurred to him that she smelled of baby shampoo, like a child. Then she fished in her desk drawer to find a hand mirror to admire the effect. 'Thank you, Daniel,' she said, blushing as she looked up at him through her lashes. 'It's a very special gift and I'll treasure it always.'

'Good,' he said, clapping his hands, anxious to get back to business. 'Foxie thought you'd like it.'

At the mention of Foxie, Pepper's smile faltered. 'But I'm already having a holiday, aren't I? You didn't need to bring me a present as well.'

'You're welcome.' He shrugged, wondering how much more simple life might have been if he'd followed his original plan and taken his PA to New Zealand instead of Foxie who had turned his world upside down as she always did, leaving him with a kaleidoscope of mixed emotions. But when he saw Pepper looking up at him with adoring blue eyes full of hero worship, he decided he might have had a lucky escape.

Foxie's first impression after driving home was that absolutely nothing had changed. She walked into the house to find Marion and Rose drinking coffee after lunch, getting ready to put their feet up for the afternoon to watch a movie on TV, unable to decide if it should be *Chicago* or *Moulin Rouge*.

'All right for some.' Foxie grinned at them. 'I've got to make sure Jim's ready to accommodate three more horses.'

'Only three?' Marion said, looking disappointed. 'The trip was a waste of time, then?'

'Not at all. We thought it better to start

small and iron out the wrinkles as we go along. Soon as we know the system works without too many hitches, we'll go back for more. For now we have two nice fillies and a really handsome colt. Wait till you see him, Mum, he's really special.'

'And how did you get on with Daniel?' Marion shot a mischievous glance at Rose. 'Manage to get through the week without biting each other's heads off?'

'Actually, yes, we did.' Foxie gave them a bland smile, although she knew the two older women were dying to hear more. 'Any chance of a cuppa?'

'Darling, of course.' Marion sprang to her feet. 'What am I thinking of? You must be parched.'

While Marion bustled away to make it, Foxie picked up the magazine from last week's Sunday paper. She had seen Rose's speculative look, but she wasn't ready to get into a heart to heart with Daniel's mother. Not yet. She needed to be certain of Daniel's feelings first, as well as her own. In New Zealand, away from the pressures of home, it seemed so right that they should get back together. Now she wasn't so sure. Maybe Daniel expected her to see it as a holiday romance — a pleasant interlude but not to be taken too seriously.

Idly, she flicked through the magazine, expecting to find the usual mix of fashion and celebrity gossip until a spread in the centre pages stopped her in her tracks. On one side there was a flattering full page picture of her mother on the window seat, looking out into the garden and on the opposite page a montage of her own baby photographs leading up to the present day with a glamorous publicity photograph of herself as Carole Parker. She saw the words had been written by Clare Mallis. And if that wasn't bad enough, the two main headlines made her cringe, *Carole Parker's Mum Tells All*, and in smaller print but just as deadly, *Did you know Carole is frightened of spiders?* Foxie gave a snort of disgust and flung the magazine across the room at the same moment that Marion returned from the kitchen with tea things on a tray.

'Oh, you've seen it already, have you?' Marion's face fell. 'I wanted to show it to you myself as a nice surprise.'

'A surprise!' Foxie was almost choking with exasperation. 'What were you thinking, Mum? Telling that dreadful woman all that stuff about me?'

'She wasn't a dreadful woman at all,' Marion said defensively as she set down the tray and started to pour the tea, avoiding

Foxie's penetrating gaze. 'She was very discreet, very kind. Said how much she admired you and how she didn't want to drag any family skeletons out of the cupboard — '

'I'll bet.'

'Well, I believed her. She said she just wanted the little things — you know — where you went to school and what you were like as a child.'

'Fine, but did you have to tell her how I feel about spiders?'

'It was something to say, that's all.' Marion grew plaintive. 'And what possible harm can it do?'

'I don't know yet,' Foxie said ominously as she retrieved the magazine to look at the article again. 'We'll have to wait and see. I hope she paid you for telling her all this rubbish?'

'Not yet,' Marion said in a small voice. Suddenly, her face crumpled and she burst into tears. 'I'm sorry if I did wrong,' she said between sobs. 'But I enjoyed talking to her and I really thought you'd be pleased.' Overcome by her emotions, she hurried from the room and seconds later they heard her running upstairs.

'Oh, Foxie, did you have to?' Rose said, looking pained. 'I've been working so hard to keep her positive and amused. It's still only

months since she lost your father. Emotion-
ally, she's still very fragile, you know.'

'I do know,' Foxie groaned at herself. 'Me
and my wretched temper. I should've
remembered how she is.'

'And I did try to warn her about talking to
reporters. I've been in hot water with Daniel
over the same thing. They seem to be so
sympathetic and all on your side until you see
what they've written and find out they were
after something else entirely.'

'I'll go up and apologize. Take her some
tea. I'm a beast. I didn't even give her the
present I brought.'

'Don't beat up on yourself.' Rose smiled.
'I'd leave her alone for now. A jolly good cry
won't hurt her. I'll check on her in half an
hour and take her something if she isn't
asleep.'

'Thank you, Rose.' Foxie hugged her.
'What would I do without you?'

'Finish your tea before you go and see Jim;
it's raw out there. And you might as well
check your mail at the same time. There's
been quite a bit of it while you were away.'

Foxie leafed through a few bills and a pile
of fan mail forwarded from the studio and set
it aside. The only items that interested her
were a small parcel and a letter from
Cameron Carstairs; she recognized his

156

expensive vellum. It had to be important or he would have sent an e-mail. Inside, she saw that it was a personal letter written in his own sloping hand. Too private even to trust to his PA.

He wrote: Jane. How does the saying go? Missing you already. Well, we were missing you even before you left. The show merely limps along without you and the ratings are so bad, we're being overtaken by every other soap in the business. Is there the slightest chance you'd like to come back? We would always find a place for you.

As what? Foxie smiled, remembering the storyline of a car exploding with Carole Parker inside it. A long lost twin sister or my own ghost? She supposed clever writers were capable of getting out of tight corners, particularly those who wrote soaps, but to resurrect Carole Parker would be asking a lot of any audience. She blew out a long breath and read on.

I shall be in Australia for a few weeks, Sydney and Melbourne, on a mission to find a new Aussie teenager to bring into the show. It would be great to catch up, even if you're happy with your decision and don't want to come back. I'll call you when I arrive. Kindest thoughts, all best, Cameron.

She looked at the postmark on the envelope and frowned. It had been posted two weeks ago, which meant that Cameron might already be here. She folded the letter carefully and tucked it away in her handbag. If she herself found it unsettling, her mother would find it even more so and she didn't want her to come across it accidentally.

Then she gave her attention to the parcel. It was about the size of a large matchbox. Addressed to Carole Parker, but to her own home address here, it had not been forwarded from the studios like most of her fan mail. It had been posted from Melbourne and had been sitting waiting for her for over a week.

She unfastened the wrapping and found that there was indeed a large matchbox inside. She looked for a note to explain it but found none. The box was quite light and as she shook it, something brittle rattled inside. Suddenly, she had a premonition that she didn't want to open it and set it aside. Rose saw her hesitation.

'What's the matter, Foxie?' she said gently. 'You've gone quite pale.'

'It's this parcel,' she said. 'I don't know what it is, but I'm having a feeling I don't want to open it.'

'Do you want me to open it for you, then?'

'Yes. No, of course not. I feel such a fool, Rose. Scared of what's in a matchbox. It can't be a letter bomb. It would have gone off as soon as I opened the package.'

'A letter bomb?' Rose looked shocked. 'Why on earth should anyone want to harm you, Foxie?'

'Oh, I had a few threats when Carole was at her destructive worst. Some went far enough to threaten to kill me.'

'But that's ridiculous. Surely people realize it's only TV?'

'Not always.' She gave a shaky smile. 'Some of them think it's for real.'

'Well, let's settle it once and for all,' Rose said briskly as she opened the box and cautiously peered at the contents, holding it at arm's length. 'Ugh,' she said, recoiling from the sour smell before she closed it and put it aside. 'I don't think you want to see this, Foxie. There are dead insects inside.'

'What sort of insects?'

'Not insects exactly, they're spiders,' she said and hastened to add as Foxie recoiled in horror. 'Don't worry, they're all dead. Two poisonous redbacks and a huntsman. What a horrid practical joke.'

'Somebody must've sent them after they saw that article in the paper. They're only dead because I wasn't here and the parcel waited all week. Lucky me, eh?'

'Dear me. I can see fame has its drawbacks.'

'Doesn't it just? And to think I had a letter from Cameron today, actually inviting me to go back to LA.'

'Foxie, you wouldn't.' Rose looked stricken. 'Your mum would be heartbroken to say nothing of — ' She broke off, biting her lip.

'Nothing of what?'

'Never mind.'

'You don't have to worry. Going back to LA is the last thing on my mind. But Rose, you're not to mention any of this to Mum?'

'If you don't want me to, no,' Rose said, although she looked troubled.

'And you won't tell her about that nasty little parcel, either?'

'I'll get rid of it now in the Aga.'

'Thanks. I'll go and see Jim.'

Feeling the need of a soothing breath of fresh air on the way to the stables, she followed her usual routine of checking the pensioners in the back paddock. This time she was shocked to find at least half of them missing, only the oldest and most infirm left behind. Already upset by the parcel, she set off for the stables with some stern questions to put to Jim. She found him in his office, looking harassed.

'I know, Miss Marlowe,' he said, addressing her formally for once. 'I know what you're going to say but it wasn't my fault.'

'Just tell me they're not dead. I'll never feed Witherspoon pet's meat again if they are.' She put a hand on the head of her father's old dog who had come up to greet her, pushing his nose at her hand.

'Dead? Lor', bless you, no. We had this offer, you see, from a new riding school — '

'A riding school?' Foxie raised her eyes heavenwards. 'Come on, Jim. These are ex-racehorses, not ponies or hacks.'

'Yes, but these people know what they're doing. They want them for experienced riders — not kiddies.'

'But won't they be too skittish? Some of them haven't been ridden for years.'

'I know. But Mr Morgan thought — '

'Daniel again,' she said through gritted teeth. 'I should've seen his hand in this from the beginning.' She turned on Jim again. 'So why wasn't I consulted or even told?'

Jim blew out his cheeks, looking embarrassed. 'I dunno. Got too many bosses, haven' I? I dunno what to do to please you all.'

'Oh, Jim, I'm sorry. But it was such a shock. I thought they'd all been sent to the knacker's yard.'

'Your dad's old pensioners? Get away. You know I wouldn't have nothin' to do with that.'

'And you did mention that if they didn't suit, the horses could come back?'

'Not in so many words, no.' Jim started looking uncomfortable again. 'But I'm sure — '

Foxie clicked her fingers. 'Give me the phone number, quick. I need to speak to them.'

She waited, humming impatiently, as the telephone rang endlessly at the other end. There wasn't even an answering machine, offering to take a message. Just as she was about to hang up, it was answered by a young woman's breathless voice.

'Blacklocks. Tina speaking.'

'And this is Jane Marlowe from Marlowe's Racing Stables.' She knew she sounded unfriendly but she couldn't help it.

'Oh, right, Ms Marlowe,' the girl said cheerfully, seeming to know who she was. 'You'll be wanting to know how the old boys are settling in?'

'Matter of fact it was rather a shock. I only just found out the old boys, as you call them, were gone.'

'Oh.' The girl didn't seem to have an answer for that.

'I'd like to speak to the owner of Blacklocks, please. Is that you?'

'My father. But he isn't here right now. Is there any way I can help you?'

'Maybe. You see, we have an emotional attachment to those old horses.' Foxie's voice faltered as she found herself close to tears. 'And if I'd been consulted, they would never have been sold.'

'Really, Miss Marlowe, I hope I can set your mind at rest. Your horses have settled as if they've been living here all their lives. They seem delighted to be back doing useful work.'

'You're not pushing them too hard?'

'Look, if you're worried about them, please come out and see us. We're only ten kilometres away, after all. Any time between five and six; we always have our horses in before dark.'

'Thank you, Ms Blacklock, I will.'

'Oh, call me Tina, please. I'm only eighteen.'

Feeling better after her conversation with Tina, Foxie went to make her peace with Jim. But she was still angry with Daniel for selling off half the old pensioners without telling her.

While they were deciding where to house the new arrivals, the telephone rang again.

This time it was Harvey Watson, looking for Foxie.

'How was New Zealand?' he asked without preamble.

'Fantastic. Successful in every way.'

'Good. But that's not really why I rang. Foxie . . . ' The solicitor hesitated as if he wasn't quite sure how to put it. 'You haven't paid any funds into Morgan Enterprises, have you?'

'No,' she said slowly, wondering what he was getting at.

'I'm happy to hear it.' Harvey sounded relieved.

'But I have dipped into my savings to buy a promising colt for $110,000 as my contribution to the new business.'

'A hundred and ten thousand dollars for one horse?' Harvey sounded as if he were about to have a stroke.

'No ordinary horse, I promise you. Dangerous Red is a very special colt.'

'So who owns it, then? You or Mr Morgan?'

'Both of us. I told you. It's my contribution to the business. Why? Is anything wrong?'

'I sincerely hope not. But I've been hearing a few things about your Mr Morgan since last we spoke. His father was something of a rogue.'

'You can hardly blame Daniel for that.'

'No, but you know the saying. The acorn never falls far from the tree.'

'Just what are you getting at, Harvey?' Foxie felt her cheeks beginning to burn. 'Stop talking in riddles.'

'All right. Morgan always operates the same way. He'll take over an ailing business for next to nothing, make it viable again and then he'll sell it on, usually at a handsome profit.'

'So? That's not much different from buying a run-down house, doing it up and selling it on at a profit.'

'I'm not saying there's anything wrong or illegal about any of it. But how will it strike you when he tires of building up Marlowe's Racing Stables and wants to sell that on at a profit?'

Foxie felt a cold shiver travel down her spine. 'He wouldn't. He knows what it means to Mum and to me.'

'And have you taken any steps to prevent it? So far, you have bought him a very expensive horse. Do you have anything in writing to protect that investment?'

'No,' she said in a small voice, biting her lip as she heard Harvey sigh at the other end.

'I'll draw up some contracts for you both to sign, protecting your interests, but it's probably too late. He already has what he wants and it's hardly in his best interests to let you in as a partner now.'

'I'm sure he will. We have verbal agreement already.'

'Well, I hope you're right.'

'Harvey, you're talking as if Daniel's done something wrong and he hasn't. I was the one who fell in love with the colt and I chose to buy him. I was happy to spend the money because I knew he was right for us.'

'Oh? And did Morgan himself buy some horses costing over $100,000?'

'No.' Foxie said slowly. 'He bought two fillies at twenty thousand each.'

'Ha,' said Harvey Watson. 'I rest my case.'

8

Angry and unsettled as she was, Foxie's heart still skipped a beat when she answered her mobile and heard Daniel's voice.

'Get home safely?' he asked, sounding warm and encouraging as ever, not at all the voracious wolf in sheep's clothing that Harvey would have her believe. 'I was hoping you'd ring me to say so.'

'Were you?' she said, unable to keep the edge from her voice.

'Foxie, is everything OK there? You sound a little distracted.'

'Well, I've had one or two unpleasant surprises since I came home.' She started telling him what was on her mind. 'Why didn't you say you were selling those horses to Blacklocks? That's OK. I can answer that for myself. You knew damned well that I wouldn't let you, that's why.'

Daniel's mood changed as soon as he sensed her hostility. 'It was a business decision, that's all. Extending the working life of horses no longer of use to us. And I know the Blacklocks — they're good people. They know how to look after their stock.'

'Fine, Daniel, but that isn't the point. Those horses were my father's old champions and not yours to sell.' Her voice faltered and once more she felt close to tears.

'Foxie, I know you have a sentimental attachment to those horses but we need to be practical here. We can't run a viable business on sentiment. I thought we were partners on equal terms. I don't expect to have to clear every decision with you.'

'Oh? And when you tire of building the business here at Marlowe's and want to sell it, I suppose I'll be the last to know?'

'Whatever gave you that idea?' He seemed completely taken aback by her outburst. 'Who on earth have you been talking to? That crazy old lawyer of yours, I suppose.'

'Harvey's not crazy, he's very astute. And he always has my best interests at heart.'

'And I don't?' He sounded as much hurt as exasperated. 'It's always the same with you, Foxie, isn't it? I've never known a woman to be so changeable, so capricious. One moment we can be friends, lovers even, but all it takes is one wrong word from someone to bring it all crashing down. There has to be trust between us or else there's no point in carrying on.'

She knew he was right but she was too much on her high horse to climb down. 'I still say you shouldn't have sold those old horses without telling me. I'd never do such a thing without telling *you*.'

'All right, all right, you've made your point. But what else has happened? You might as well tell me. You said you'd had more than one unpleasant surprise?'

'Oh, nothing really.' She didn't feel like telling him about the matchbox and the spiders; he'd only start binding on about his friend with the hypnotist. 'Mum's been talking to a reporter and she got upset when I told her off.'

'Now I can sympathize with that. Rose used to chatter her head off to anyone who would listen till I set her straight. Maybe it's not all bad. The stables need all the free publicity we can get.'

'That's what Mum said. But I can't see how an article by Clare Mallis on the childhood of Carole Parker will be any help to anyone.'

'Clare Mallis? Oh, no.'

'Oh, yes. All the same, we probably got off lightly. But you didn't ring here just to hear me grizzle. What's up?'

'No. This time it's good news. Ten people have put their hands up for the shares in Mighty Minnie and we decided to have a maximum of six. We'll have to put all the names in a hat and pull out the winners. Then we can offer the others some shares in the New Zealand horses if they're still interested. All happening, isn't it?'

'Sounds like it.' Foxie was smiling again, caught up in his positive mood. 'Oh and Daniel — '

'Yeah?' he said softly.

'Sorry I jumped down your throat before.'

'Think nothing of it,' he said, not entirely in fun. 'If you were nice to me all the time, I'd think you were ill. Foxie, if you really don't like it, I can ask Blacklock to let me buy those horses back. He's a nice old chap and I'm sure he'll understand.'

'No, don't do that. Not until I've gone over to see them. Tina says they fit in as if they've been living there all their lives. I don't want to disturb them if they really are happy to be back in work.'

'That's settled then.' He sounded relieved.

'So when can we expect to see you down here?'

'Very soon. Our first syndicate members will want to look over their investment in the flesh. We need to have an open day with a buffet lunch — not at your house,' he hastened to add, hearing her gasp of dismay. 'We'll hire a tent and have outside caterers of course.'

'You had me worried for a moment. I'm allergic to aprons and you wouldn't want to rely on my cooking. When d'you want it to be?'

'On a Sunday, I think, soon as poss. Jim's going to moan as usual and make all the excuses in the world, but he'll just have to get over himself.'

'I'll warn him if you like so it won't be too much of a shock. Was there anything else today?'

'No, not really, Foxie, I — '

'Then I'll be seein' ya, Daniel,' she said brightly and hung up.

He sat there staring at the phone for a long moment after she'd gone and running his fingers over the Victorian tooled leather ring-box in his pocket. It contained his grandmother's ring; a lozenge-shaped emerald surrounded by diamonds and in a fine gold filigree setting. He had just collected it from the jeweller where he had sent it to be cleaned, reset and brought back to life. He opened the box and looked at it for a moment, watching the stones almost mocking him in their splendour as they caught the light. Then he sighed, shook his head and put it back in the drawer where it had been lying since he inherited it some years before. He had made the mistake of rushing things with

Foxie before and wasn't about to do so again.

The seven days in New Zealand had been pure magic, more wonderful than in his wildest dreams. They had seemed so compatible, so completely at ease in that country setting. But now they were home again with their feet on solid ground, he didn't need to see her face to face to know that the kaleidoscope of her emotions had taken another turn and things had changed between them yet again.

In his mind's eye, he had seen how their open day could have been. In front of everyone, he would have placed his grandmother's ring on her finger and she would have accepted the applause and congratulations with tears in her eyes. But that wasn't to be. Until she could trust him completely and was no longer swayed by the opinions of people like Harvey Watson, the ring must remain hidden away.

★ ★ ★

Two weeks later, Pepper returned from the Gold Coast sporting a light tan and a spiky new haircut which made her look younger than ever. Daniel had to look twice to make sure it really was his PA and not another new temp on loan from the agency.

'I do so *love* the Gold Coast,' she enthused. 'It's a whole different world up there. I had the best time ever.' She gave a secretive smile like a cat who has just licked cream, giving Daniel the impression that there had been more to this holiday than just surf and sun.

'Do I take it there's a new boyfriend in your life?' he said.

'Not exactly a boyfriend.' She crinkled her eyes at him. 'He's American and quite old really, but he has the most divine accent. I could listen to it all day. He said I was exactly what he was looking for.'

'A cradle snatcher, then?'

Pepper frowned at this but didn't rise to the bait.

'I shall need you to work Sunday week,' he said over his shoulder on the way to his office. 'Double pay as usual, of course.'

'Oh Daniel, no!' This came out as a wail. 'Not next weekend — '

'It's not office work; I want you to come to a party. The new horses will be here from New Zealand and we're having an open day down at Marlowe's for existing clients and prospective new shareholders. I'll need you to help chat them up and field enquiries like you did at the races. You can bring your American friend, if you like.' At this suggestion, Pepper brightened at once. 'Who knows, he might even be interested in taking a share.'

'Oh, I don't think so.' Her face fell and she started fiddling with some papers on her desk, suddenly unwilling to meet his gaze. 'He'll be going back to the States quite soon.'

Daniel stared as his PA. It occurred to him that she seemed very young, vulnerable and possibly in need of protection. She didn't say much about her family, but he gathered that most of them lived in the country, in New South Wales. He could only hope this American, whoever he was, wouldn't break her heart.

★   ★   ★

After visiting the Blacklocks and meeting both Tina and Ron, the owner of the riding stables, Foxie's mind was put to rest. She scarcely recognized her old pensioners whose coats had been groomed until they gleamed, instead of being allowed to grow shaggy and wild in the paddock. Back in work again, they had lost weight and looked to be in much better shape than at home. Seeing them like this, bright-eyed, alert and keen to be useful again, she felt more than a little ashamed of her outburst towards Daniel. Maybe she would be able to make it up to him when she saw him again. She thanked the Blacklocks and invited them to the open day at Marlowe's.

'We'll be there — won't we, Dad?' Tina accepted for both of them, although her father remained silent, frowning and scratching his chin. 'He's a proper old hermit,' she whispered to Foxie. 'It's over five years since Mum died, but I still can't get him to go anywhere.'

'Come on your own then, if he won't.' Foxie smiled back, having taken to the pretty, dark-haired girl. 'It'll be a good day and there's sure to be someone you know.'

★   ★   ★

On the Sunday morning in September set aside for their big day, Foxie awoke in the early hours to the sound of persistent rain. Listening to it pattering on the roof, she turned over and groaned. The day was going to be a disaster. Who would get out of bed to drive down to the coast in the midst of a thunder storm, to spend the day paddling about under an umbrella, looking at horses in the rain? No one would come and they would have to eat caterers' sausage-rolls and pies for a fortnight.

But her fears were unjustified. By breakfast time a light breeze had blown all the clouds away and the sun was high in a clear, if wintry, blue sky.

Daniel had arrived about half past eight to join them for breakfast, dressed in jeans but wearing an expensive Italian jacket that looked as if it had been tailored specially for him. It made him look like a gentleman farmer, Foxie thought. She herself had dressed to look the part as well, wearing jodhpurs, a vintage brown leather aviator's jacket from the seventies, set off with a man's white silk evening-scarf. She was wearing the minimum of make-up and her newly trimmed hairstyle gleamed.

'Wow!' Daniel had teased when he saw her. 'You look like Amelia Earhart minus the goggles. Who would ever believe that you don't like to ride?'

'And you're not to tell them,' she warned.

Although Jim took pride in making sure both the stables and the animals in his care were kept in first-class condition, he had excelled himself today. Every casual employee had been roped in to help and the tack gleamed, hanging in orderly rows on the walls. Every stall was fragrant with clean sawdust and each horse's smelly offering was removed as soon as it was presented.

The tent had been set up in one of the paddocks near the house and the caterers arrived promptly at 10 a.m. with trestles, tablecloths and a portable kitchen from which they would serve the food.

At midday, when the first visitors were expected, Marion and Rose took up a station under a brightly coloured market-umbrella at the front gate, ready to direct people to the tent where Foxie and Daniel were waiting to greet them. They had decided to prime their guests with food and wine before introducing them to the horses.

Pepper was late, which didn't improve Daniel's temper and by 12.15, he was pacing up and down, glancing at his watch. So far only Aunty Jo had arrived, looking funereal in her best black and smelling of mothballs. Thankfully, this time she had left her excitable Yorkshire terrier at home. She stood in the entrance to the tent and gazed around before she folded her arms, getting ready to criticize.

'Really, Foxie,' she said. 'I don't know why you had to go to all this expense.' She waved a dismissive hand towards the caterers. 'I could have made a few cauldrons of my cock-a-leekie stew. Much healthier than all this pastry.'

'Cauldrons, indeed,' Foxie muttered, giving Daniel a sly wink. 'We wouldn't put you to all that trouble, Aunty Jo. You're here to enjoy yourself. Have a glass of wine and sit down.'

Jo accepted a glass of sweet sherry and for once did as she was told.

'Do you think anyone's coming at all?' Daniel muttered through gritted teeth, eyeing Jo as if she were a bad fairy who had come expressly to keep everyone else away. 'Where the hell are they?'

'They'll be here,' Foxie told him. 'Have a glass of wine yourself and calm down. It's a Sunday, remember, and everyone gets up late. Nobody wants to be the first to arrive.'

The words were no sooner out of her mouth than four cars drew up at the front gate and people spilled out of them, laughing and eager to start enjoying themselves. It was Barry Glenn, the television presenter, along with his party of friends and hangers-on. He thumped Daniel on the shoulder and kissed Foxie before introducing the rest of his party.

'We're just punters, really, and don't know anything about horses,' he confided. 'But we're all very willing to learn.'

After that the visitors came thick and fast, including Tina Blacklock and her father, and soon the tent was filled with the buzz of conversation as the guests stood or sat around eating finger-food and enjoying wine.

Pepper arrived at last, pink-cheeked and murmuring apologies to Daniel for being so late. He accepted them with a cool nod and then turned towards her escort, waiting to be introduced. A balding man in his late thirties, he couldn't be anything other than Californian because of his clothes, too light and summery for an early spring day in Melbourne.

But before Pepper could open her mouth to say anything, Foxie spoke up instead.

'Cameron Carstairs! What on earth are you doing here?'

'Jane! My, but you look wonderful. Well rested and younger than ever.' He stepped forward to greet her with a kiss on both cheeks and a hug, making Pepper frown like a sulky child. 'But didn't you get my letter? I wrote and told you I was on my way to this part of the world.'

'Well, yes. But for some reason I didn't expect you just yet. Or to see you with Pepper.' The tactless words were out before she could prevent them.

'Ah well, you see,' Cameron put a fatherly arm across Pepper's shoulders to draw her in. 'Pepper here is a special case. She's going to be my — '

'Cameron, wait,' Pepper interrupted him urgently, pressing a hand to his chest. 'I haven't told anyone yet.'

'Told anyone what?' Daniel said tightly,

picking up on it immediately and staring at Cameron rather than Pepper. 'This is all rather sudden, isn't it? I hope you know she's only nineteen?'

'And looks even younger now I've persuaded her to cut that long hair.' Cameron added enthusiastically, entirely missing the threat in Daniel's tone.

Fortunately, at that moment, a waiter arrived with a tray containing glasses of red and white wine as well as champagne. Daniel took a glass of red wine and drained it while the others accepted flutes of champagne. Foxie looked from Daniel to Pepper and back again. Was she the only one to notice that he seemed unusually put out over Pepper's involvement with Cameron Carstairs?

Later, when Daniel had spirited Pepper away and pressed her to work, she took her chance to have a few words with Cameron alone.

'What are you up to, you wicked man?' She teased. 'Don't you know that Pepper is Daniel's treasured PA?'

'So? She can't let that stand in the way of her future. I have big plans for that girl.'

'Come off it, Cam. You can't be in love with her. You've only known her a couple of weeks.'

'In love?' For a moment Cameron looked

dumbfounded and then he burst into delighted laughter, hardly able to speak. 'Jane, you're priceless. You can't possibly imagine that I — ' He roared with laughter again and it was some time before he could control himself. 'Of course I'm not in love with her, any more than she is with me.' He took out a fresh handkerchief, wiping tears of mirth from his eyes. 'Pepper Harcourt is my new Australian discovery — I'm offering her a part in the show.'

'But what makes you think Pepper can act? She's a secretary, a PA.'

'Lots of girls who want to act have been trained to do office work.' He adopted a mocking falsetto. 'Mama says they must have *something to fall back on if it doesn't work out*. But seriously, the girl has talent — she auditioned for me on the Gold Coast and won the part over fifty others. I'm sure she's going to be an asset to the show.'

Foxie frowned, watching Daniel working his way around the other side of the tent and wondering how he would respond to this latest blow.

'But never mind about Pep, that's a done deal. Right now I'd rather talk about you.' Cameron was making the most of having Foxie to himself. 'Is life in the country panning out as you expected or is it — ?' He left the question hanging in the air.

'Is it what?'

'Beginning to pall? Maybe you've had enough of playing the dutiful daughter and would like to come back to us, after all?'

'Get real, Cam.' She giggled. 'Carole Parker died in a car that exploded after falling off a cliff. I don't see how she can possibly come back.'

'Easy. We can say someone pulled her from the car just before it went over.'

'Oh? And what about the funeral? The cremated remains?'

'That can be explained, too. A carjacker hiding behind the driver's seat. She didn't get out.'

'A carjacker?' Foxie wrinkled her nose. 'But where has Carole been all this time? And don't you dare say amnesia, the fans won't buy it.'

'Well, I don't know. That's a problem for the writers, isn't it? Just take it from me, we'll find a way round it if you want to come back.'

'Cam, it's nice to be wanted and I'm flattered of course but — '

'You're getting ready to say 'no' and I won't let you. Not yet. I'll be in town for another week or so before I need to get back. Take some time to think it over and if the answer is still 'no' when I'm ready to leave,

'I'll accept it with good grace.' With a conspiratorial wink, he went in search of Pepper.

After an extended lunch and when everyone was feeling expansive, Jim and his lads put Mighty Minnie through her paces, showing her off to her new co-owners. She even allowed them to rub her nose without trying to bite, although Jim kept her on a tight rein, aware that she could be upset by noise and crowds.

The newcomers from New Zealand were praised and exclaimed over, Barry Glenn and his friends demanding to take all of the shares in Dangerous Red, who had been in training already and might well be a candidate for one of the stakes races in the lead-up to the Spring Carnival.

There was only one sour note for Foxie during the whole day and that was when Pepper brought some people over to her while she was having a quiet moment alone, taking a breath of fresh air outside the stables.

'Foxie, these people have been dying to meet you all afternoon.' Pepper made the introduction hastily without even waiting for her to turn round. 'Frank Patterson and his wife, Stella.'

Foxie took a deep breath, found her professional smile and turned to greet the

Pattersons. But the smile fell from her face immediately when she recognized Stella Patterson as the plump woman who had tried to ruin their evening at the Chinese restaurant.

'Hi there, Carole. We meet again.' Stella bared her teeth in a smile that didn't quite reach her eyes, taking advantage of Foxie's discomfiture to get in first. 'Nice place you have here.'

'Thank you,' Foxie replied through lips that were suddenly stiff. 'But you really must get over the idea of calling me Carole. Carole Parker is just a character in a soap opera and I'm the actor who played her. If you'd take the trouble to read the credits, you'd see that my name is Jane Marlowe and — '

'Oh, I know that's what you like to be called *now*.' Stella waved a dismissive hand. 'You don't fool me. You'd like to walk away and forget all about that nice husband of yours in LA. You'd rather pretend to be someone else entirely; a woman who knows about horses.' She lowered her voice to whisper. 'Swaggering about in jodhpurs — who are you kidding? I'll bet you can't even ride.'

'I can so.' Foxie heard her voice rising in panic as she stared around hoping someone would come to her rescue. Pepper had

184

disappeared into the tent and the more serious clients were still inside the stables with Daniel and Jim. 'You really must excuse me. I have to see to my other guests.'

'Not before I get some answers.' Stella placed her bulk squarely in front of her, blocking her path.

'Now, Stella,' Frank piped up in a reedy voice, clearly ill at ease with his wife's obsession. Ineffectually, he tried to take her arm and pull her away. 'Leave Ms Marlowe alone. You don't want to start making another scene.'

Stella shook him off almost sending him flying. 'No, Frank. I mightn't get another chance to catch her alone like this.' Once more she lowered her voice, leaning forward until her face was inches from Foxie's, making her recoil from the mingled smells of lipstick and sour breath. 'How did you like the present I sent you?' She raised a hand and wriggled her fingers before Foxie's eyes. 'Did they tumble out of the box and run all over your desk?'

Foxie gave a small scream and pressed the back of her hand to her mouth, making Stella laugh.

By now Daniel had joined them, quick to take in Foxie's terrified expression. 'Are you all right, Foxie? What's going on here?'

She shook her head, eyes wide.

'Your wife is upsetting Ms Marlowe and not for the first time,' he snapped, addressing his remarks to Frank Patterson rather than Stella. 'I think you should both leave — now. We're cancelling your application to become shareholders and we don't expect to see you anywhere near here again. Our staff will be warned not to admit you to any part of the complex and if you do return the police will be called.'

'I'm so sorry,' Stella's husband was in an agony of embarrassment, almost wringing his hands. 'When she told me she wanted to come down here to see horses, I thought she was getting over this stupid obsession. All she can ever talk about is *The Brave and the Free*. I just don't know what to do with her any more.'

'Nor do I, Mr Patterson. If I were you I'd get some professional help.'

Frank nodded.

'I'm not going to see any shrink and you can't make me.' Stella was raising her voice and refusing to budge as a small crowd gathered around them to see what the fuss was about. 'This is just a plot to discredit me. You're all in it together.'

'Stella, please.' Once more her husband tried ineffectually to make her see reason, but his wife remained with her hands on her hips, her feet planted even more firmly on the ground. Daniel called over two of the lads and instructed them to help Frank Patterson manhandle his wife into their car. She was still waving her arms and screaming abuse when they fastened her into her seat like a naughty child.

Daniel stood with a supportive arm around Foxie whose legs were still trembling. Without speaking, they watched the car until it left the driveway, gained the main highway and was lost to view.

'How the hell did those two find their way here?' he said, giving Foxie a reassuring shake. 'Most of our guests came by invitation only.'

'She must have seen that article in the Sunday magazine,' Foxie said dully, without thinking.

'Did she say so?'

Foxie shrugged, not wanting to mention the parcel of dead spiders that Stella expected to run out of the box as soon as it was opened.

'Well, don't let it get you down. Everyone else has enjoyed themselves and the day is a great success.' He started leading her back towards the tent. 'What you need is another glass of champagne.'

'Oh no, Daniel, I really don't — '

'Yes,' he said, getting a fresh glass and pressing it into her hand. 'I'm not letting you run away into the house to hide. Even Ron Blacklock has finally come out of his shell. Look at him over there with your mother.'

Foxie looked and indeed Ron Blacklock seemed to be in the midst of an animated discussion with her mother and Rose. She took a sip of champagne and began to feel better. Daniel was right; she ought not to let the Pattersons spoil her afternoon.

Later, when all the guests and even the caterers had gone, leaving nothing behind but the empty tent, they sat around the kitchen table with their mothers and Jim, comparing notes. Everyone agreed the day had been a resounding success. Even Aunty Jo had gone home smiling.

'And Dangerous Red looks like paying his way already,' Daniel said. 'Barry Glenn and his mates are very taken with him.'

'What about the New Zealand fillies?' Foxie asked.

'There won't be much interest there till we have something to show for it,' Jim said. 'Reckon we'll have to work 'em up ourselves like we did with Minnie.'

Daniel nodded. 'They might be hanging back now but the punters will be fighting each other to come aboard soon as one of them wins a race.'

After supper, Daniel stifled a yawn as Foxie walked him to his car.

'I hope you're not too tired to drive home,' she said. 'You know you'd be welcome to stay.'

'Oh yeah?' He gave her a cheeky grin. 'And have our mothers lying awake all night listening for footsteps pattering along the corridors.'

'I doubt it. They're exhausted enough to sleep like logs, the pair of them.'

'Mm. So what are you suggesting?' He moved in closer until she was very aware of his nearness, his tall body pressing against her own.

'Nothing, of course.' She smiled, breaking the tension. 'I'm completely exhausted myself.'

'You think so now,' he gave her a light kiss on the temple. 'But in half an hour or so — '

'Daniel, stop teasing me.'

'OK. OK.' He stood away from her. 'Fancy Pepper getting herself involved with your American friend. The long arm of coincidence, eh? Let's hope she's planning a long engagement.'

Foxie looked away thinking it wasn't up to her to tell Daniel the true nature of Pepper's business with Cameron. No doubt Pepper would do so in her own good time.

'What's up?' he said, sensing her tension and change in mood. 'Aha. You don't like it, do you? Pep taking up with your old boss.'

'No, no, it's not that.'

'What, then? I hate it when you get all secretive.'

'I'm not being secretive!' she said through gritted teeth.

'Well, you know the guy better than I do. What's wrong with him, then? Big time TV producer — he must have been married before?'

'Uhuh. Three times.'

Daniel winced. 'Three times already. Poor little Pep. I hope she knows what she's getting herself into.'

'I think poor little Pep, as you call her, is a lot more cunning and astute than you give her credit for. I'm sure she can manage her life very well without Uncle Daniel wading in with his big boots to save her.'

Daniel stared at her for a moment and then his face creased into a delighted smile. 'Foxie Marlowe, I do believe you're jealous. Jealous that I'm concerned about an innocent girl who happens to be a long way from family and home.'

'I won't dignify that remark with a civil

answer. Of course I'm not jealous,' she said, turning her back on him and starting to walk away. 'Goodnight to you, Daniel Morgan.'

She was halfway to the back door when he caught up with her, swinging her easily into his arms and almost lifting her off her feet. Before she realized what he would do, she found herself being thoroughly and excitingly kissed. She resisted for only a moment before relaxing into it and enthusiastically kissing him back. It was some time before they came up for air.

'Come back to town with me now,' he whispered. 'We don't need to tell our mothers. They'll know where we've gone.'

'Daniel, I can't. Jim worked so hard today; I gave him the day off tomorrow. I'm supervising the horses at first light.'

'OK. Drive up on Tuesday then. We have a lot to celebrate.'

'Maybe. But it's still early days. There's a lot of hard work to be done, especially with those fillies. You can't just buy a good-looking horse and expect it to win by instinct.'

'And you think I don't know that?' His eyes showed a flash of temper. 'I've probably spent more time around horses than you have.'

'Then why don't you stay the night here and help us out in the morning?'

'Can't. There's a guy coming over from

191

Adelaide with a view to buying the fitness complex.'

'You're selling the fitness complex already? But you can't have had it more than three or four months?'

'Three and a half, actually. But it's as good as I can make it.' Daniel shrugged. 'So in my book it's ready to go. I get bored with things once they're up and running and there's no more planning to be done.'

Foxie stared at him, reminding herself of all Harvey Watson had said. How long would it be before Daniel was bored with his present commitment to Marlowe's and wanted to sell it on? In the light of this latest news, it seemed that the threat was all too real.

'What's the matter now? You've got a glazed look like a rabbit caught in the headlights,' Daniel teased. 'Not still worrying about that silly Patterson woman, are you? I can send a couple of security guards to keep watch on the place if you are.'

'What?' She had scarcely heard what he said. 'Oh, there's no need for that. I'm sure her husband will take your advice and get help.'

'She should be committed. Righto, then. Since I can't stay and you won't be tempted to come with me . . . '

'I can't. I made a promise to Jim and I have to keep it.'

'Then there's nothing more to be said than g'night.' He gave her the lightest possible kiss on the lips and was gone, getting into the car with scarcely a wave. He didn't look back.

9

And when she walked back into the house still mulling over what Daniel had just told her, she received more news for which she was totally unprepared. With a glance at Rose to see if the timing was right, her mother stopped her just before she could wish them goodnight and slope off to bed. She wanted to be alone to collect her thoughts.

'Darling, can we have a word before you go up? Rose has some news — or rather we both have news that we don't want to keep from you any longer.'

Instinctively, Foxie knew this was something that she didn't want to hear. Not right now while she had so much else to worry about.

'Can it wait till the morning, Mum?' She glanced at her watch. 'I'm whacked and I've given Jim the day off tomorrow. I have to get up at the crack of dawn with the lads.'

'Well, that wasn't very forward-thinking, was it?' Marion said sharply. 'You must've known you'd be exhausted after today.'

'Well, Jim is exhausted, too,' Foxie

snapped, her patience running out. 'And it's too late to change it now.'

'All right, you two,' Rose said gently, realizing that if the argument were to escalate it would end in tears. 'Foxie, I promise this won't take long, but we can't keep it to ourselves any longer. I've had such a good offer for my cottage that I've decided to accept it and move on.'

'You're not selling Rose Cottage?' On the heels of what Daniel had told her, Foxie was so shocked, she blurted the words. 'But you've had it for years — it's even named after you. And what about your garden, your lovely roses?'

'Well, that's why they want it, of course.' Rose shrugged, using much the same mannerism as her son. 'I can always start again with some new ones, if I want to, although roses don't do so well in Queensland. I might try my hand at hibiscus instead.'

'You're moving to Queensland?'

'Yes. I'm buying a unit overlooking the beach on the Gold Coast. Fabulous views. And the warmer weather will suit my arthritis the doctor says.'

'But what about Mum? She's going to miss you terribly.'

Here Rose and Marion exchanged glances like children caught out in a prank.

'I won't have to miss Rose at all.' Marion smiled. 'Because she has asked me to go and share her new home with her. To begin with, I wasn't so sure but talking to Ron Blacklock helped me to make up my mind.'

'Ron Blacklock? But you'd never met him before today?'

'I know and I feel so sorry for him. His wife died over five years ago and he can't seem to get over his grief and move on. The house remains just as she left it — he won't even let Tina dispose of her clothes.'

'That's awful. But I don't see what that has to do with you.'

'No? You see, I feel the same. This house has become a place of too many memories. I still sleep in the bed I shared with your father. And when I'm not thinking, I walk into a room, expecting to find him there.'

Foxie sat on the arm of her mother's chair and, taking her hand. 'It's early days yet, Mum — only a couple of months. You can't expect these feelings to disappear overnight.'

'I'll never get over them, not while I'm living here. I shall end up in a time warp like poor Mr Blacklock.'

'All right, let's look on the practical side. What will become of this house if you go? Will you sell it or what?' After Daniel's news about the fitness centre, suddenly it seemed to Foxie as if the whole world was built on shifting sands, everyone in the process of selling up.

'Of course I won't sell it. It's your inheritance. Your father and I agreed that when you married and took over the business, we should pass it to you.'

'I'm not planning on getting married any time soon.'

'You don't have to pretend with us, dear.' Marion glanced at Rose. 'We saw you and Daniel kissing just now.'

'You were spying on us?' Foxie sat up straight, withdrawing her hand.

'Not at all. You were standing out there in the open for all to see.'

'We're not living in the dark ages, Mum. There's a world of difference between kissing and getting married, you know.'

'Oh.' Marion looked crestfallen. 'But after you came back from New Zealand, I thought . . . ' Once more she glanced at Rose. 'We both thought . . . '

'Well, I'm sorry to disappoint you in your matchmaking but you thought wrong.' Foxie stood up and faced them, temper on the rise. 'And we're certainly not going to marry just to suit your convenience. Matter of fact, I'm not sure I want to get married ever!' With that parting shot, she swung out of the room, letting the door bang so loudly behind her, the ornaments rattled inside her mother's china cabinet.

And later, although she had gone to bed expecting sleep to claim her as soon as her head touched the pillow, she couldn't help replaying the scene in her mind. What was wrong with her? Why had she overreacted like that? It wasn't as if she didn't love Daniel, she knew very well that she did. It was *his* feelings she was uncertain about. And now he was selling the fitness centre, confirming everything Harvey Watson had said.

If only Marion and Rose would stop matchmaking and leave them alone, they might work things out for themselves in their own good time.

Then, on top of all this, she started to worry about Marion trying to live in a tropical climate. Heat waves in Melbourne left her listless and prone to headaches. How was she to survive in Queensland where the summers were relentlessly long and hot?

When her alarm went off at 4 a.m. reminding her it was time to get up and organize the boys with the horses, she sat up, rubbing eyes that felt gritty and sore. She felt as if she had scarcely had any sleep at all.

★ ★ ★

'What do you mean you're leaving for LA in less than a fortnight?' Daniel thundered, making Pepper cower and stare at him, wide-eyed. She had seen him in a temper before, but never as angry as this. 'Of all the hare-brained ideas. Don't you know America has a strict immigration policy? You can't just get on a plane and go; you'll need to have visas and work permits in place before you leave.'

'Cameron says he can arrange all that; he's done it before.'

'And as for starring in one of his wretched soap operas. Ludicrous. Whatever makes you think you can act?'

'I can so.' Pepper lifted her chin to defy him. 'And anyway, Foxie didn't have all that much experience when Cameron gave her a chance.' She saw at once that this was the wrong thing to say as Daniel's scowl deepened. 'This is something I've always wanted to do. Cam says I'm a natural, a breath of fresh air.' Her employer answered this with a snort of derision. 'Don't be mean, Daniel. You're only cross because you'll have to train someone new.'

'No. I won't be training anyone, you will. Pronto. And if I'm cross, it's because I know you'll only make a fool of yourself and get thrown out in less than a week. Get real, Pep:

you're a good PA. Why not stick to what you know?'

'*You* don't. You're always trying new things. But you expect me to stay on as your devoted, old-fashioned secretary until I'm a dried up old stick like Miss Thing at the bank in *The Beverley Hillbillies*.'

Finally, he recovered his sense of humour and laughed, shaking his head. 'You see, Pep. You always know how to tease me out of a bad mood. How can I possibly manage without you?'

'Easily. You managed perfectly while I was away.'

'For a week or so, yes. But . . . '

She put her head on one side, considering him. 'All right. If I'm all that irreplaceable, I might be tempted to stay — on double pay, of course.'

'Cheeky baggage! No. Go and tilt at your windmills. You can always come back if it doesn't work out.'

★   ★   ★

After supervising the training of the horses, pleased to see the newcomers getting used to the local track, Foxie was feeling surprisingly refreshed and alert as they ambled home, the boys chatting happily amongst themselves.

She was leading Dangerous Red who was calm and biddable once he had exercised. At the same time, she had the feeling that she was superfluous; the boys knew exactly what had to be done, even when Jim wasn't there. Simon Grant had come to put Dangerous Red through his paces and he was impressed with the colt who had clocked up some formidable times, leaving his racing partner many lengths behind. No other horse in the stable had such speed and stamina and she was excited at the thought that thanks to her investment, they might have a champion in the making.

Back at the stables, still not feeling up to making apologies to her mother and Rose, she drank tea with the lads and stayed to help them water and feed the horses. And when the phone rang in Jim's office and nobody answered it, she picked it up herself, to be greeted by pips indicating that it was a long distance call.

'Hello, Marlowe's,' she said automatically, expecting it to be someone looking for Jim. She was answered by the gruff voice of a man who sounded as if he smoked too many cigarettes. She could imagine him sitting there with a fedora pushed to the back of his head like a gangster in an old-fashioned film noir.

'Lookin' for Danny. Is the boy there, luv?'

Foxie frowned. One thing she knew about Daniel was that he hated his name to be shortened to the common diminutive. 'No, he isn't' she said. 'Mr Morgan usually conducts his business from his office in town. I can give you the number if you — '

'Already tried there an' missed him. Thought he might be down at the stables with you?'

'Afraid not. But I can take a message, if you like?'

'Douggie Boulter here of Boulter Brothers, callin' from Sydney. You can tell him I'm getting tired of waiting. He'd best pull his finger out an' get those contracts back to me double quick if he's still interested in goin' ahead.'

'What contracts?' Foxie felt as if a trickle of ice had travelled down her spine.

'Never you mind, lass. No business of yours.' The man gave a wheezy chuckle that turned into a cough, making Foxie hold the phone away from her ear until he had finished. 'Don't you worry, love. If you're a stablegirl, your job's safe enough. We'll still need good people in Melbourne. But tell him to get on to it, quick smart. Can't wait forever. Got that?' And without waiting for her reply, he was gone.

Speechless, Foxie stood with the telephone receiver clamped to her ear, long after the line had gone dead. Then she put it gently back on the hook as if she thought it might bite. There was all the evidence she needed to know that Daniel had been planning to betray her all along. She closed her eyes against a wave of sickness and anger against herself. To think she had almost fallen for him all over again.

Slowly, she walked back to the house and let herself in quietly through the back door. She didn't want to see her mother or Rose until she had settled the turmoil in her mind. Was it possible that Rose had known about this, too? Had she been a party to it, aware of her son's intentions all along? Surely not.

Upstairs, she changed quickly from her jeans and sweater into a tight-fitting black gabardine suit that reflected her mood. She grabbed her mobile and her handbag and made for the stairs, shoes in hand so as not to make a noise. Fortunately, she still had the keys to the station-wagon, so she wouldn't have to ask Marion's permission to take the car.

But her mother waylaid her before she could reach the front door. White-faced and with dark circles under her eyes, Marion looked as if she hadn't slept much either.

'Oh, Foxie,' she said with a tremor in her voice. 'Where are you off to now? We really do need to talk. I shouldn't have let Rose spring it on you, like that. We had no idea you'd be so upset.'

She stared at her mother for a long moment and then dropped her handbag to sweep her into a warm embrace.

'No, Mum. It isn't your fault. You and Rose have every right to plan a future together — why shouldn't you? It's just that it came as a shock on top of everything else.'

'What else?'

'Nothing for you to worry about right now. But that's why I'm going to town. To see Harvey Watson and try to sort everything out.'

'That sounds rather ominous.'

'I'll know more when I've seen him. I also promised to look up Cameron Carstairs before he leaves town.'

'The TV producer? I hope he's not trying to persuade you to go back to America?' Marion was unusually perceptive. 'Rose says Daniel's fit to be tied over losing Pepper.'

'I'm sure,' Foxie said, not without bitterness. 'Perhaps it'll do him good to lose something for once.'

'Now what's all *that* about? I just know there's something you're not telling me. I hope you're not rushing off at a tangent again without being sure of your facts.'

'I'm sure of the facts, all right, if I can believe my own ears. The big question is how much did Rose know?'

'About what? You're scaring me, Foxie. I wish you'd just tell me what's going on.'

'No time now. Half the morning's gone already. I'll tell you everything when I get back. Promise.' With that, she gave Marion a quick peck on the cheek and ran for the door.

'But Foxie . . . ' Marion called after her, realizing as she did so that it was too late. Her daughter was already driving towards the main road. She stood in the doorway, trying to make sense of the little she had been told.

⋆ ⋆ ⋆

Her first setback was to find Harvey Watson away from his office.

'I'm so sorry, Miss Marlowe,' Miss Beech, his elderly secretary consulted her diary. 'I didn't know you were expected today.'

'I wasn't. I just thought . . . '

'He'll be so sorry he missed you but he's spending the whole day in court with the barrister, looking after the paper work. If only you'd telephoned first to say you were coming.'

'No. It was a spur of the moment decision.

I realize now I should have made an appointment.'

'Maybe I can help. Your journey might not be entirely wasted.' The secretary rose and went over to Harvey Watson's desk to look through a pile of papers awaiting his attention. 'Ah, yes. Is this what you came for? We had the contracts returned from Mr Morgan's solicitors yesterday. All you need to do is to sign them yourself and Mr Watson will see to the rest.'

'No way. Far as I'm concerned, they're not worth the paper they're written one. You might as well tear them up,' she told a shocked Miss Beech. 'Tell Harvey I'm extricating myself from Mr Morgan's clutches before I lose any more of my savings.'

'Oh, I wouldn't do anything hasty, Miss Marlowe. Not until you've seen Mr Watson. I know he was anxious to talk to you himself.'

'I'm sure.'

'Give me your mobile number again and I'll get him to call you as soon as he can, although it might not be today.'

'Thanks.'

Outside the office, she stood for a moment, wondering what to do next. She hated the thought of a wasted journey and didn't want to go home with her queries unanswered.

Deciding to leave her car at Harvey's office,

she headed across the bridge from the city towards the offices of Morgan Enterprises on the other side of the river. Although it was spring, the wind was bitterly cold and she pulled her fashionable jacket around her, wishing she'd worn a coat and a scarf instead. She was shivering by the time she reached Daniel's office.

'You can't see him now.' An anxious Pepper confronted her, quick to observe Foxie's stormy expression. 'He's with a visitor from Adelaide.'

'Selling his new fitness complex,' Foxie said through gritted teeth.

'Well, yes. But how did you — '

'I know a lot of things. And I gather congratulations are in order. I hear Cameron Carstairs is taking you back to LA to star in his show.'

'Yes, isn't it wonderful?' Pepper's eyes sparkled with excitement. 'I've always wanted to act on television, to be famous.'

'You'll find out it's not all it's cracked up to be; there's no time for a social life. And Cam's a hard taskmaster; I ought to know. He'll have you worked off your feet from dawn until dusk.'

Pepper bit her lip, for once looking less than certain. 'He said he was sure I'd rise to all of the challenges.'

'Well, you're young and eager, why not?' Foxie managed a smile. Just because she was angry with Daniel, it wasn't fair to take it out on his defenceless PA.

Just then the door to his office opened and he came out, ushering an older man before him.

'Foxie! What a nice surprise.' He turned, introducing her to his visitor. 'Tom Freeman, this is my partner, Foxie Marlowe.' He really did seem genuinely pleased to see her. 'I thought you were busy at the stables today?'

'Oh, I was.' She acknowledged Daniel's guest with a formal smile. 'But I'm afraid something came up. Something that can't wait.'

'Ah,' he said, catching the ominous inflection in her voice. 'I'm sorry, Tom,' he said to his guest. 'But you know how it is when a lady says it can't wait.'

'I do, indeed.' Tom gave an indulgent smile to Foxie, setting her teeth on edge. 'I'll go on down to the pub and wait for you there.'

'Thanks. I won't be long.' Daniel gave him a grateful clap on the shoulder and held open the door of his office for Foxie to go inside. 'Oh and Pepper,' he said almost an afterthought. 'You might as well grab half an hour for lunch.'

'Now?'

'Yes, now,' he said. 'I'll need you to hold the fort while I'm out with Tom.'

He waited, making quite sure Pepper was leaving before closing the door to give Foxie his full attention. 'Now, then,' he said, moving into her space as if he intended to draw her into an embrace. 'Tell me about this something that just can't wait?'

She pushed him away so hard he stared at her in shock. 'Foxie! What's that all about?'

'Don't come the injured innocent with me. You can't pretend you don't know!' She was so angry, she could scarcely get the words out.

'OK, I can see you're upset. But how can I put it right if you won't tell me what's wrong?'

'Oh, stop sounding so bloody reasonable, you snake! You're selling us out to Boulter Brothers, aren't you? Just as you intended to do all along.'

His eyes widened in shock. 'Where on earth did you get that idea?'

'From Douggie Boulter himself. He called the stables, didn't he? Wanted to speak to his old mate, Danny Boy.'

Daniel nodded, taking a deep breath. 'Foxie, if you'll calm down and listen to me for a moment, I can explain.'

'He did that already. It seems you're

holding him up on some contracts he wants you to sign.'

'Exactly. That's just the point.'

'All right, Daniel. I need to know one thing only and then I'll leave you in peace. Have you been negotiating with Boulter Brothers to sell them my father's stables?'

'Yes. Yes, I have. But that was — '

'Thank you so much. For being honest with me at last.' Heart thumping and beginning to shake with rage, she could scarcely see through her tears to get to the door.

'I've always been honest with you, Foxie.'

'Oh, sure.'

'You can't do this. You can't leave without giving me the chance to explain.'

'Watch me. I don't need your explanations, it's clear as day. Rose is selling up, going to Queensland and taking my mother with her. How convenient is that? Very soon John Marlowe's racing stables won't even exist; they'll be part of Boulter Brothers' Melbourne operation. The one thing I don't understand is why did we have to go to New Zealand? Why did you let me buy Dangerous Red?'

'You know that already. We'd lost a lot of horses and needed new blood, to — '

'To do what? Make it more enticing for

Boulter Brothers? Encouraging them to pay more?'

He stared at her as if he had just woken from a long sleep, slightly bemused, as if he were seeing her for the first time. 'I can't talk to you while you're like this. You've made up your mind I'm the villain here and you won't hear a word I'm saying. Foxie, go home. I'll talk to you when you're more rational.'

'When I'm more rational? When you've had time to cook up a good story, you mean.' She raised her hand as if she might strike him but he didn't flinch or avoid it. He just stood there, holding her with his gaze.

'Go on, then. Hit me, if it makes you feel any better.'

Suddenly her temper evaporated, leaving her drained and exhausted, ashamed of her shrewish behaviour, however justified. Slowly, she lowered her hand and turned towards the door.

'We can't go on like this, Foxie.' He sounded as weary as she felt. 'With no trust between us. Every time something goes wrong, you think I'm to blame.'

'Daniel, just do whatever you want,' she muttered, without looking back. 'I can't care any more.'

Somehow she found herself outside the office, hailing a cab and giving the driver the name of a luxury hotel at the top of town. It wasn't far and under normal circumstances, she would have walked, but her legs felt like jelly and she needed to dry the tears that streamed down her face and redo her make-up before facing the TV executive. Cameron was a man whose life was filled with glamorous women and she didn't want to arrive looking like a dishevelled, emotional wreck.

'Cameron Carstairs,' she said to the young man at reception. 'I believe he has a suite.'

'Who shall I say is here? I'll check if it's OK for you to go up.'

'It will be.'

'I have my instructions, madam. I must ask you to wait while I check.'

'Jane Marlowe,' Foxie said, rolling her eyes heavenwards and tapping her foot as he made the call. A moment later, he smiled and nodded. 'Mr Carstairs says you can go on up. Suite 33 on the top floor. He says you've just caught him, he was on his way out to get a late lunch.'

The lift shot up to the top floor with such speed, it made her feel a little queasy. Before getting out of the lift, she checked her reflection in its mirrored walls, thankful to see that she looked like herself again with no trace of her recent emotional upset.

The door to the suite opened just as she was about to knock.

'Jane, come in, come in.' Cameron greeted her with a kiss on both cheeks, ushering her inside. 'Welcome to my Melbourne abode.' He looked her up and down, taking note of her black suit. 'Aren't we a little sombre today?'

'I was feeling sombre. I had some business to attend.'

'Oh?' he said, unusually perceptive. 'So all isn't perfection in the world of the horse?'

'Far from it,' she gave a wry smile.

'Does this mean I can hold out some hope that you're changing your mind? That you're thinking of coming back to us?'

'Maybe yes, maybe no. I need to know what you're offering first.'

'The starring role, of course. What else? I've already had the writers work up some new ideas — for you and for Pepper.'

Foxie almost gaped. 'You really were that certain I would come back?'

'Not at all. But we work up a whole lot of story lines so that we're never caught without something to shoot. We've also got several new characters waiting in the wings. Some of them we won't even use.'

'You mean there are some actors who won't get their chance if Carole Parker returns to the show?'

'Don't even think about them. Dashed hopes and rejection are part of an actor's lot.'

'You don't include Pepper in this?'

'No, no. We have great plans for her, whether you come back or not. She is to play the part of Carole's long lost biological daughter come from Australia to track down her mother — '

'Hold it right there, Cam. She could be my younger sister, yes, but a *daughter*? She can't be more than nine years younger than me.'

'That don't matter. Think of it, kid. It'll be wonderful. Our established Australian star makes a comeback together with the new Australian kid on the block.'

While she was still speechless with shock, he started to look at her critically, head on one side, then he walked right around her, inspecting her as if she were a slave he might buy. 'You'll need longer hair of course; we can't have it short. Should be several shades lighter, too. We can always get you some extensions while it grows. An' we'll book you in to a health farm for a week of intensive weight loss. You need to drop three kilos at least.'

'Excuse me?'

'Carole might be a mummy, but we can't have her looking like one. If you're three kilos over now, the camera will increase it to six.'

Foxie stared at him and then she started to laugh, her laughter escalating until it was almost hysteria and she couldn't stop.

'What?' he said. 'What did I say that's so funny?'

At last she got herself under control, wiping her eyes and ruining her mascara before noisily blowing her nose, watching Cameron frown at these little human frailties.

'I'm so sorry, Cam. I thought I could come back and do it all over again, but I can't. I don't want to starve to lose weight in a hurry nor do I want to play the mother of a 19-year-old girl. It's all just too hard.'

'No, no it's not.' He started talking faster as she continued to shake her head. 'Listen to me, Jane. You can do it and it'll be great. Anyway, I won't let you say 'no' till you've seen the script.'

'I don't need to. After ten years, I could almost write one myself.'

'Yes! We'll give you artistic input; you can even direct an episode, if you like.'

'Cameron, listen to me. I am saying 'no' and this time you have to accept it. I was so angry with everyone here, I thought I could turn my back and walk away from all of it, but I can't. I can't let my enemies win. I have to stay and fight for the business my father wanted me to have.'

Unused to defeat, Cameron was no longer smiling. 'This is the last time, Jane. Reject my offer now and it's the end of the line. There'll be no changing your mind again and no coming back.'

'I understand,' she said. 'No hard feelings, eh?'

He grunted, his scowl deepening. Spoiled and used to getting his own way, he didn't care to be thwarted.

'The man at reception said you were going to lunch. Will you let me treat you, for old times' sake?'

'I'm not hungry now,' he said, his mind running on other things. 'And if you're sure you're not coming back?'

'Quite sure.'

'Then I'll need to make some calls to the States.' He turned towards the telephone and asked for an outside line without even bothering to see her out. So far as he was concerned, she had already gone.

Foxie walked out of the suite, feeling she'd made the right decision. On the way to see Cameron, she'd almost convinced herself her best option was to return to the show and take up where she left off. But that would mean losing her own personality to become Carole Parker again. And the TV producer's arrogant certainty that she would obey his instructions had made her rebellious. She had been her own woman for several months now and liked it that way. She didn't want to live on celery sticks and starve herself down to a size eight again, she didn't want the chore of coping with long hair and she certainly didn't want to play the part of Pepper Harcourt's mother! How Daniel would laugh if he knew about that. Her inner smile faded as she remembered Daniel's betrayal; she wouldn't be sharing jokes with him any more.

* * *

When Foxie left his office, Daniel sat down at his desk again, in no hurry to rejoin Tom Freeman. The man was pleasant enough and had already agreed to pay Daniel's asking price for the fitness centre without trying to beat him down, but he seemed far too interested in Daniel's private life. This had been a mystery to Daniel until Tom produced a family photograph and pointed out his youngest girl. Daniel made all the right noises although the girl was the image of her potato-faced father.

'I want to move the whole family over from Adelaide, but Lucy's digging her heels in. If only I could introduce her to someone like you and you'd do me the favour of taking her out to dinner once or twice — just until she finds her feet in Melbourne and gets settled in.'

'I appreciate your dilemma, Tom, but I really don't think I'm the man for the job.'

'Nonsense. I know you're not married. Not serious with anyone, are you?'

Daniel was tempted to say it was absolutely no business of his but remembered the deal was sealed only on a handshake, having yet to be signed, so he restrained himself with a tight smile. 'I *was* involved with someone until quite recently. Not sure I'm over it yet.'

'Then Lucy's the one for you! She has the kindest heart in the world.'

Fortunately, having said this, Tom let the subject drop and their conversation returned to matters of business.

Daniel sat there staring into space until the office clock reminded him that it was after half-past two and no lunch would be served after three. He hoped Tom would have ordered ahead of him because after the scene with Foxie, his appetite had completely deserted him.

10

As soon as she returned from the city, Foxie went to see Jim to tell him of Daniel's plans. 'And don't pretend this is the first you've heard of it.' She leaned across his desk, accusing him. 'Otherwise you'd be more shocked.'

'I'm sorry Miss Marlowe.' Jim always addressed her formally when he felt under threat. 'Some months ago when, you know, when your father . . . ' he felt awkward speaking about John's death. 'Well, I happen to know Mr Morgan only came in because his mother asked him to an' he warned us at the time that he still might have to sell out to Boulters if he couldn't turn things around. But of course that was before — '

'Before what?'

'Before you came home. With a Marlowe at the helm again, we thought everything was going to be all right.'

'Far from it. The latest I hear is that old Mr Boulter really is licking his lips and getting ready to take over. He thought I was one of the stablegirls, even told me my job would be safe.'

'That's right.' Jim rubbed his chin, looking anxious. 'Everyone's job will be safe except mine. Boulters are a tough crowd and I know how they operate. They'll keep on the grooms and lads because the horses are used to them but the stable foreman is always a man of their own.'

'Oh Jim, I'm so sorry. I wish there was more I could do.'

'I'll be all right. There's always someone lookin' for a man of my experience and with a trainer's ticket as well. The missus might kick up a bit about movin' an' takin' the kids away from their school, but we'll get around it somehow.'

'Oh, Jim.'

'Worse things 'appen at sea.' He moved some papers about on his desk, embarrassed by her concern. 'We hear your mum's going to live up north with old Mrs Morgan, so where does that leave you, lass?' he said gently. 'I suppose you can always go back to LA?'

''Fraid not. I've already burnt that particular bridge. I'm here and this is where I shall stay until Boulters get someone to serve me with an eviction order. I've got the lawyers on to it and we're not going down without a fight.'

'Good for you, lass.' Jim tried to smile but she knew it was all bravado.

★   ★   ★

Over the next few weeks, Foxie went through life waiting for the axe to fall. Daniel stayed away, keeping in touch with Jim via lengthy phone calls. It was difficult for her to plan ahead, let alone keep her mind on the day to day work of the stables. One of the new fillies from New Zealand was already showing some promise but the other one couldn't get used to the barrier stalls and kept rearing inside the gates. Until she could overcome this problem, it would be impossible to enter her in a race.

Dangerous Red, with several minor wins under his belt, was entered for one of the country cups. If he were to succeed there, it might even earn him a place in the Caulfield Cup.

But each day she awoke, expecting to hear the wheezy tones of Doug Boulter on the phone, informing her it was all over and that the business was now his.

Harvey Watson, shocked to hear of Daniel's treachery, had agreed to investigate all avenues, to see if he could find a way out. But although he communicated with her almost daily, he could only confirm what she already knew: that Daniel's purchase from Marion was legal and indisputable. Money had changed hands at the time and Harvey could find no loophole to let them out.

All too aware of Foxie's resentment towards her son, Rose made herself scarce and returned to live in her cottage until it was sold. She told Marion the sale was due to finalize any day and she needed to pack as well as dispose of some heavy furniture that she didn't want to take with her up north. The flat was light and airy, she said, more suited to cane tables and comfortable basket chairs than the antique Victorian pieces she had once loved.

Marion herself spent hours dithering over her built-in wardrobes, still full of clothes going back to the fifties. She hated to part with anything and Foxie's attempts to help her always ended in arguments and tears.

'Be reasonable, Mum,' she said at last, holding up a full-length camel coat, bought during a holiday in Europe. 'You've never worn this in Melbourne yet, so what makes you think you'll need it in Queensland?'

'But Foxie, that was from Harrods. Look at the quality.'

'Quality won't count for much when the silverfish have chewed their way through it in Queensland. Some of these things are worth money. Why not sort out some of the better things and let me take them to a vintage recycle shop? At least then you'll have some money to buy what you really need.'

'I don't want to sell anything,' Marion was close to tears. 'I have very happy memories of wearing these clothes.'

'You said you didn't want to live in a time warp like Mr Blacklock.'

'I know what I *said*,' she snapped.

'Then why not let me do it for you? That way you won't have to see what I'm giving away.'

Marion pushed the wardrobe shut with a bang. 'No, thank you,' she said. 'And I'll do my own packing as well. If I left it to you, I'd be going to Queensland with nothing but a swimsuit and a pair of shorts.'

Just then the telephone rang and Marion picked it up. Moments later her expression changed, her face flushing with pleasure. 'Yes, yes,' she said, glancing at Foxie. 'Of course I can't speak for Jane but I'm sure she'll be delighted . . .'

'Delighted about what?' Foxie said in an urgent whisper. She knew that air of conspiracy; Marion was capable of committing her to something that wouldn't delight her at all.

'Do you want to speak to her now?' Marion held out the phone to Foxie who frowned, shaking her head. 'I'm so sorry, she was here a moment ago but she's just stepped out. I'll pass the message on to her and get her to call you back.' Quickly, she scribbled a number on the notepad beside the phone and turned to face Foxie, her face alive with enthusiasm.

'It's wonderful. You'd never guess in a million years.'

'Come on, Mum, I know you of old. You had the same look on your face when you tried to send me to ballet class when I was seven. *You'll love it*, you said. All I can remember is some harpy shrieking instructions in French and trying to force my feet into unnatural positions.'

'Oh stop it. This isn't anything like that. They want you to be one of the faces of the Spring Racing Carnival.'

'Oh really? Who dropped out?'

'What do you mean?'

'Mum, hello! It's September already. They wouldn't have left it this long to organize their first choice. It's far too important an event. That means somebody must have dropped out.'

'Well, they did say something about one of the *Desperate Housewives* and the girlfriend of a jockey who got suspended but I wasn't really paying attention. I was much too thrilled that they thought of you.'

'It's not exactly flattering to be third or fourth choice.'

'Now don't start. It'll be wonderful. And you won't be alone. They're trying to get Nicole Kidman if she isn't filming.'

'She will be.'

'They're employing several dress designers and a milliner exclusive to you.'

'A milliner?' Foxie groaned. 'You know I hate wearing hats.'

'Then tell them to make some of those fascinator things that just perch on your head.'

'They won't. They'll want me to wear something that looks like a UFO rising out of a wreath.'

'There'll be a stylist assigned to you as well as someone to choose your shoes. Oh go on, Foxie. Do call them back now and accept before they go and ask someone else. It'll be fabulous. I can't wait.'

'Have you forgotten? You're not going to be here for the Melbourne Cup this year. You'll be in Queensland.'

Marion dismissed this with a wave of her hand. 'Oh, I'm sure Rose won't mind leaving the move until after the carnival. Isn't it exciting? You'll meet lots of new people, too.'

'Mum, I'm not at all sure I want to do this. I'm trying to get myself taken seriously in the racing industry. It won't help my cause to go prancing around like a bimbo in flowery dresses and silly hats.'

'Why do you have to pour cold water on everything? I should be so proud and this might be my last Spring Carnival for some years.' She gave a theatrical sob. 'If you won't do it for yourself, you might at least do it for me.'

'All right, I'll speak to them. But I'm promising no more than that.'

Half an hour later, seduced by a velvet-voiced man on the phone, Foxie had agreed to make four appearances over the carnival, including the day of the Melbourne Cup. The organizer had been so sure that she would accept and fall in with his plans that saying 'no' simply wasn't an option. Not only was she to be paid handsomely just for showing up but, as a bonus, she would be allowed to keep all the clothes she was modelling too.

'Well?' Marion said when she came off the phone.

'Nice guy, but I told him I couldn't do it,' Foxie teased. 'He quite understood.'

'You told him nothing of the sort!' Marion gave her a light smack on the shoulder. 'I was listening and I didn't hear you say anything but *yes*.'

＊　＊　＊

In spite of her misgivings, Foxie enjoyed choosing her clothes: two outfits for each day; one for fair weather and one for foul. Spring weather in Melbourne was far from predictable; it could be hot as summer one day and raining like winter the next. For Cup Day she had a dark purple dress with a dramatic matching cape if it should be cold and a frothy silk georgette floral gypsy dress if the weather was hot. Cleverly, the shoes and hat had been chosen to suit either ensemble.

The milliner, disappointed that one of the few people tall enough to wear one was refusing a picture hat, nevertheless came up with an Arabian-style pillbox that sat forward and flattered her hairstyle, having no brim to catch the wind.

Contrary to her expectations, she also enjoyed the photo shoot for the Melbourne paper's Racing Carnival magazine, surprised to find herself on the cover rather than one of the models.

Two weeks later, since there was still no news from Boulter Brothers, she decided to let sleeping dogs lie and get on with her life. With several races behind him which he had won effortlessly, Dangerous Red was entered to race in the Cranbourne Cup. Cranbourne had a wide course which would suit his swooping style of winning a race. As a newcomer from New Zealand, the punters knew little about him and he wasn't highly favoured, having been lightly raced.

Foxie drove across to Cranbourne in the station wagon, following the float, and on reaching the course was directed to park near the members' enclosure while Jim and the grooms drove round to where their horse was to be stabled. Her heart lurched when she recognized Daniel's Mercedes among the parked cars. It hadn't occurred to her that he might be here.

She took a deep breath, squared her shoulders and marched up the stairs to the members' enclosure, grateful that she had taken some care with her appearance today; she knew she looked crisp and fresh in her mint-green linen suit. Even in a room full of people, she was aware of Daniel at once, seated drinking coffee with Barry Glenn and his cronies. Barry spotted her and waved her over.

'Hello, my lovely,' he said, greeting her with a theatrical kiss on both cheeks. 'And looking more gorgeous than ever. How's our horse, today? Is he ready to win?'

'Maybe,' she smiled. 'But don't crow about it too loudly, you'll shorten the odds.' Finally, she acknowledged Daniel with a brief smile and a nod.

'Foxie,' he said, equally cautious and unsmiling.

'Let me get you a coffee.' One of Barry's friends got to his feet. 'Or, if it isn't too early, champagne?'

'It's too early for me,' Foxie smiled. 'But don't let me stop you.'

'There'll be time enough time for champagne when we've won the Cup.' Barry said, taking no heed of Foxie's earlier warning. 'Lets go down and have a look at our boy.' Leaving Foxie and Daniel in awkward silence together, he stood up and left, his friends trooping behind him. Clearly, they were used to Barry calling the shots.

'I didn't expect to see you here today,' she said to Daniel when they were alone.

'Why not? We're still partners for the time being at least. We should show a united front to our clients.'

'A united front, indeed! I'd no idea you could be such a hypocrite.'

'It isn't hypocrisy, Foxie, it's just good business sense. At least until we can work something out.'

'How do you do it, Daniel?. You always make me feel as if I'm in the wrong.'

He gave his characteristic shrug. 'Maybe

this time you are.'

She felt her cheeks redden as her temper rose. 'I'm not the one selling out to Boulter Brothers. It's bad enough that you'll do it to me but what about Jim who's been loyal to the stables for so many years? Forcing him to make changes at his time of life.'

'I'm not forcing Jim to do anything.' He sounded weary. 'But you're too pig-headed to let me explain.'

'Try me,' she said. 'I'm all ears.'

'Not now, Foxie. This isn't the time or the place.'

They were sitting there glaring at each other, aware of no one around them until another voice intruded, sharp and clear as cut crystal, making them both start.

'Well, well. If it isn't the love birds. Cosy up a little and give us a snap, you two.' It was Clare Mallis, her photographer in tow, eyes glittering with pleasure as she realized she had caught them in a private moment and off guard. 'I do hope I'm not intruding on a lovers' tiff?'

'Not at all,' Daniel responded with a tight smile. 'We were just talking business.'

'Oh, business,' she said with a dismissive wave of her hand before turning her attention to Foxie. 'I gather congrats are in order; you've landed a plum job as one of the faces of the Spring Carnival. Lucky you. Nothing to do but swan around in borrowed plumes and drink champagne all day. Your mother said you were so busy, I'm surprised you can find the time.'

'I'll manage,' Foxie said, not wanting to give the woman enough ammunition to write another article.

'And which persona? Jane Marlowe or Carole Parker?'

'Far as I'm concerned, Carole Parker is dead and I hope she stays that way.' She was trying to give as little as possible, hoping the woman would take the hint and leave.

At a signal from Clare and before Daniel or Foxie could arrange their faces into a suitable pose, her photographer fired off a series of shots and gave her the thumbs up that he had what she needed. Uneasily, Daniel and Foxie watched as they moved on to somebody else.

'Now what's she going to make of all that?' Daniel muttered. 'And who the hell gave her the idea that we're love birds?'

'Three guesses.' Foxie closed her eyes.

'I don't need them. Your mother, who else?'

Foxie nodded. Somehow, the discovery of a common enemy in Clare Mallis, had defused some of the animosity between them, although Foxie knew better than to let down her guard.

The afternoon wore on and soon it was time for the running of the feature race of the day, the Cranbourne Cup. There had been a shower or two earlier in the day, just enough to soften the track, making the ground suitable for Dangerous Red. He came out to parade in the mounting yard walking calmly beside his groom, ears pricked and interested in all that was going on around him. This time Jim had given the ride to a senior jockey, Mike Walton, to the disappointment of Simon Grant who worked with the horse every day.

By the time Daniel and Foxie rejoined Barry Glenn and his party, the TV presenter was red-faced and merry, if not well on the way to being drunk. He had been showing off, placing such a large bet on his horse that he had already shortened the odds. Jim, ever the pessimist, pulled a long face.

'Dunno what he's goin' to say to me if we lose,' he whispered to Foxie. 'There's some serious competition about today; everybody wants to win this race.'

'Remember what Dad used to say?' She grinned back at him. 'No guarantees in racing, Jim. You've done your best with the horse. No one can ask more than that.'

'They will,' he jerked his chin towards Barry and his friends. 'They think the race should be handed to them on a plate.'

232

As it happened, Jim's worries were unfounded. Although, in the early stages, Dangerous Red looked outclassed, racing at the rear of the field and having difficulty in finding the rhythm of the race, by the time they reached the home turn he had caught up with the front runners and was making a spectacular charge to the finish. For a few heart-stopping moments, it seemed as if Walton had misjudged it, leaving his run too late, but the horse was focused, intent on running everyone down and he passed his nearest rival just before the winning post to secure the race by a short head.

Barry Glenn and his team went wild. Hats were thrown in the air and Barry himself swept Foxie off her feet to whirl her around.

'We won! We won!' He yelled in her ear, almost deafening her. 'And I'll pick up two thousand smackers from the bookies, as well!'

'Then I'd get round there and claim it before the presentation, if I were you,' Daniel said. 'Wait until afterwards and you might find the guy's disappeared.'

That thought sobered Barry immediately and he raced off to the bookies' stand, his cronies lurching drunkenly behind him.

'That was a bit mean.' Foxie narrowed her eyes at Daniel. 'Why did you tell him that when you know it's not true?'

'He was enjoying himself too much, too full of himself to thank Jim or the rider. I wanted to take him down a peg.'

Foxie gave him a sideways glance, once more perplexed by Daniel's multifaceted personality. How could the same person capable of betraying her trust and who was even now preparing to sell her father's stables from under her, still make out he was angry with Barry for slighting Jim and Mike? It didn't make any sense. For the first time, she wondered if she had jumped to conclusions and acted too hastily, refusing to hear Daniel out or to let him explain. She turned towards him, preparing to offer the olive branch, when she was forestalled by a beautiful dark-haired girl who broke from the crowd to hurl herself into his arms.

'Daniel,' she ran her hands possessively through his hair, almost purring his name. 'I was hoping I'd find you here.'

'Laura,' he said, returning her hug and smiling down at her. 'What are you doing here? What a nice surprise.'

Foxie didn't wait to hear more. If Daniel had a new girlfriend already, she wasn't going to hang around to be introduced. Instead, she let the crowd close around them and made her way to the course in front of the grandstand where the presentation of the cup was due to take place.

Barry Glenn, more used to public speaking than anyone else, made such a long speech that people were getting restless and there was scarcely time for Jim or Mike to say anything, much less herself. After the presentation and feeling disinclined to run into Daniel again, she told Jim that unless he needed her, she would leave now and see him later at home.

'Not feelin' crook are you, Foxie?' He peered at her, his lined face even more shrivelled with concern. 'You look a bit peaked to me.'

'Just tired, Jim.' Somehow she dredged up a smile. 'It's been a long day.'

'But a good one,' he said, smiling back. 'We've a champion in the making there.'

★   ★   ★

On the day before the Caulfield Cup, Foxie had to go to the course for a photo shoot. The favourite, Caruso, was brought out, along with the Cup, and the local papers took a series of shots of Foxie with the horse.

She hadn't realized that one of her duties as one of the Carnival ambassadors would be to judge the entrants for the 'Fashions on the Field' contest at the Caulfield Cup, along with her designated escort for the day. Until she had arrived on course, she had no idea that this was usual or that she would be expected to spend the whole day in his company.

Her escort turned out to be Gunnar Fresk, head of a Swedish furniture factory. He had recently opened a warehouse in Melbourne to compete with his much more well-known Swedish rival. Tanned and fit, Fresk was wearing a cream linen suit more appropriate to the tropics instead of a cool day in Melbourne. Blond and good-looking in an 'action man' way, he spoke English with a strong Swedish/American accent and seemed to expect women to find him fascinating. From the smiling and lip-glossed pouting that was going on all around them, Foxie realized there were clearly many women who did. She, however, was in no mood to be charmed by any man, particularly one as obvious as Gunnar.

'I haf seen you on television,' he pronounced, nodding at her. 'Ja. An' I like long legs. Too many girls haf good bodies spoiled by short legs.'

Foxie smiled nervously, not wanting to encourage this train of thought but, Gunnar pressed on anyway.

'Afterwards, I would like you to come to

my house,' he said, taking hold of her upper arm and giving it a squeeze. 'We shall get to know one another better, yes?'

Not if I have anything to do with it, Foxie thought, raising her eyebrows and glaring at his hand until he detached it. Then she had to step aside to avoid it landing possessively on her waist.

'I think we should keep our minds on the job in hand.' She spoke sharply, nodding towards the line of contestants, trying to look elegant while keeping a tight hold on both hats and skirts to prevent them being blown about by the gusting wind. 'These girls have taken a lot of trouble with their appearance today and deserve our undivided attention. So if you're not prepared to give it — '

'Ach, I give enough, already.' Lines of ill temper settled around his mouth. 'I give prize for a race and they say you are to be my escort for today, my reward. I hope you're going to be worth it.'

Foxie was so astonished she laughed aloud. 'You have the wrong idea. I'm not *that* sort of escort at all. Like you, I am a guest of the Carnival organizers, not some tart hired for your convenience, high class or otherwise.'

'A tart? This is a cake.' He was looking puzzled.

'Oh, forget it.' She was losing patience with

him now. Fortunately, there were three girls whose outfits stood out from the crowd and with no further ado or reference to Gunnar, she chose a winner plus two others to send to the finals on Melbourne Cup Day. There they would be judged by some style guru from the States who was to be flown in specially to do so.

'I liked that blonde girl with the big mouth, the one dressed in pink,' he grumbled, as the girls started leaving the stage. 'But you don't give me a chance to say.'

'Too much cleavage and not enough fashion,' Foxie snapped back before adding mischievously. 'But you can give her a consolation prize, if you like. Why not ask *her* to come to your house.'

'Thank you, I will.' Having no idea that he was being teased, Gunnar rushed to capture the girl in pink and engage her in conversation. She seemed both flattered and delighted to receive this attention and Foxie heaved a sigh of relief, knowing she would be free of her unwelcome escort for the rest of the afternoon.

★ ★ ★

A few days later while Foxie was in the office at the stables, checking accounts, she was surprised to find she had a lot more money in her savings account than she would have expected. Further investigation revealed that her most recent deposit was in the region of $120,000 and she wondered at first if it might be an error. But it didn't take her long to conclude that this was exactly the sum she had paid to the New Zealand owners of Dangerous Red, including the auctioneers' fees and the cost of transporting the horse to Australia. The bank confirmed also that the money had come from Morgan Enterprises. Somehow, that gave her little pleasure. It meant that Daniel was salving his conscience and, at the same time, wiping the slate clean.

But how had he managed to do it? Close as they had been in New Zealand, she had made the original transaction herself and had never given him her bank account details. It didn't take her long to think of Marion.

'Mum!' She stood in the hall and called up the stairs. Her mother was still rummaging in her closets, undecided about what to keep or to give away. 'Come down here, will you. We need to talk.'

'Oh Lord, Foxie, what is it now?' Marion looked down the stairs at her daughter. Recognizing that tone of voice, she wondered what crime she had committed this time. Since Foxie had learned about Daniel and

Boulters, nothing could please her. She was like a bear with a sore head.

'Cup of tea?' Marion suggested, trying to head off to the kitchen.

'Later. Did you give Daniel my bank account details?'

'I don't know.' Marion avoided her gaze. 'I might have done. Why? What's he done now?' she said, showing some spirit at last. 'Cleaned you out?'

'Quite the reverse. He's paid me back the money I spent on Dangerous Red. All of it.'

'Well, then.' Marion raised her eyes heavenwards. 'What does the poor man have to do to please you? Nothing he does is right for you, is it?'

'He's kicking the dust of us off his heels before he sells out to Boulters, that's what.'

'Well, pardon me if I'm not surprised, after the way you've treated him. For all that he's good at making it, money has never mattered that much to Daniel. I should have thought you'd know that by now.'

'I'm afraid there's a lot about Daniel that I don't know. He's already got a new girlfriend.'

'And why not? He's an attractive man who wants to get on with his life. He can't hang around forever, waiting for you to come to your senses.'

Tears started in Foxie's eyes at her mother's casual cruelty. She pushed past her and ran up the stairs, seeking the refuge of her bedroom.

'Foxie, wait!' Marion called after her. 'I didn't mean to upset you.'

11

There was a record crowd at the course on Melbourne Cup Day because this year, instead of drowning the racegoers in floods and thunderstorms, the day had dawned fine and hot. From early morning the car parks had been filling and those who made a tradition of holding a picnic party were setting out folding tables and chairs beside their cars, preparing to make a day of it. Not just sandwiches either. Gourmet feasts were laid on, including spiced chicken, crayfish and smoked salmon. Some had even brought market umbrellas to keep from burning themselves or letting food and drink get too hot in the sun.

The Flemington roses were in full bloom, making a spectacular, natural background for the jockeys in their colourful silks, riding out on racehorses, washed and polished until their coats gleamed. Presentation was as important as running to win.

Foxie made a point of arriving early to report her unusual experience with Gunnar Fresk to the organizer in charge of events that day.

He didn't seem all that surprised to receive a complaint and, although he assured her he was taking it seriously, she could see he was biting his lips in a struggle to keep a straight face. All the same, he set her mind at rest, telling her Mr Fresk had not been invited to join them today and that her official escort would be a local man who understood the ground rules and was unlikely to make the same mistake.

She found her silky, floral silk gypsy dress to be light, feminine and easy to wear. With it, instead of the court shoes suggested by the style guru, she had chosen to wear her own gold, strappy sandals and a little gold shoulder purse. Posing for photographs at the start of the day against the background of a forest of stunning pink roses, she knew she was looking her best and hoped her escort for the day would be someone personable at least if not drop-dead gorgeous. If she were to run into Daniel, flaunting his new girlfriend, she wanted him to see that she was quite capable of enjoying herself without him.

Today, she was told she had no special duties to perform, merely to meet and mingle and explain the wagering system to any guests and overseas visitors who might need help in order to place a bet.

'Just go and enjoy yourself, Jane,' the

organizer said. 'You've already done us proud.'

'Fine.' She smiled back at him. 'So long as no one expects me to give any tips. I don't want people blaming me for their losses.'

Jim and his wife, Kerry — an unusually pretty woman with long fair hair and a cheerful disposition, in contrast to Jim's usual gloom — were taking the day off to come to Flemington. It was a tradition. Jim had not missed a Melbourne Cup Day for over twenty years. This time they were bringing Marion and Rose up from Mornington to spend the day with them.

When she first heard of it, Rose was slightly put out that Marion wanted to postpone their departure in order to stay for the Melbourne Cup, but she gave in with good grace, knowing how much the carnival meant to her friend. None of the Marlowe horses had been entered in any of the city races of that day although Dangerous Red had managed to score a place in one of the earlier races on Flemington Oaks Day in two days' time.

Foxie showed her ID and was admitted to the already crowded tent where she was to meet her escort for the day.

Her heart lurched as the first person she recognized was Daniel, standing with his back to her less than ten feet away. He was wearing a suit of such a dark blue it was almost black and he would have looked the city business-man entirely were it not for his thatch of unruly dark red hair which had grown long enough to touch his collar. He had always worn it a little longer than present day fashion decreed. She couldn't see who he was talking to, so she turned her back and moved past him, hoping that even if he caught sight of her, he would choose to ignore her, too.

'So there you are, Jane. And looking lovely today!' A tall girl she recognized as one of the organizing committee was first to descend upon her. She consulted her clipboard, pushing a pair of dark glasses back on her nose.

'I do hope you've enjoyed your time with us? We've loved having you.' She continued without waiting for Foxie to answer. 'It's such a bonus to have someone who knows a bit about horses. So many don't. Some of the models are downright scared of them,' she confided, glancing down at her list. 'But I digress. I expect you're waiting to be introduced to your escort for the day.'

'Yes, please,' Foxie said, glancing towards the organizers' table where a blond young man was standing beside it, looking ill at ease and out of place. He couldn't be more than twenty at most and seemed to be overcome with shyness. Foxie smiled inwardly. With any luck, this self-conscious, manageable boy was the one.

But the tall woman was steering her in another direction entirely, straight towards Daniel.

'Surprise!' she carolled, tapping Daniel on the shoulder and making him swing around. 'Jane Marlowe, meet Daniel Morgan, your escort for the day!'

For a moment or two, Foxie stared at Daniel, almost unable to breathe as she realized he must be equally stunned by this turn of events.

'Um, I hope it's a good surprise?' The bespectacled woman was biting her lips. 'Clare Mallis did tell me you two were an item as well as just partners. Otherwise, we wouldn't have . . . '

Daniel was first to recover. 'Sally, don't worry about a thing. It was a kind thought and we appreciate it. We'll be absolutely fine. Thank you.'

'Oh, good. That's all right, then.' The woman sighed and blushed with relief before hurrying off to attend to the next item on her list.

'Don't tell me you didn't know about this,' Foxie muttered as soon as the woman was out of earshot.

'I did not. I'm only doing it as a favour to Sally as somebody else dropped out. I thought I was to accompany one of the overseas guests.'

'Oh, yeah?' Foxie couldn't resist a moment of spite. 'Hoping for a really *desperate housewife*, were you? You should be careful. Laura might have something to say about that.'

'Laura?' He screwed up his face to look at her as if she was making no sense. 'You don't even know her. What does she have to do with any of this?'

'I dunno. You tell me.'

'Look, Foxie, if you're going to turn this into a sparring match, I'm calling a halt right now. We can catch up with Sally and tell her the deal's off.'

'Oh? For what reason?'

'We don't have to give her a reason. She'll understand.'

'Sure, she will. And go running straight to her friend Clare Mallis to spill the beans.'

'Dammit, of course she will. Yes.'

'We'll just have to make the best of it, Daniel. No matter how we really feel about each other, surely we can be civil for one afternoon?'

'I'll give it a try.' Daniel held out his hand. Foxie looked at it a moment before taking it, knowing very well what would happen if she did. All the warmth of his personality was in those strong fingers, reminding her all too vividly of what she had lost. Steeling herself for the jolt of emotion she knew must come, she placed her hand in his.

'Oh, Foxie,' he said softly, caught up in the moment just as she was and unconsciously caressing her palm with his thumb. 'Where did it all go so wrong?'

'That's easy,' she said sharply, pulling her hand free and looking him straight in the eye. 'When you showed your true colours by putting a business deal in front of everyone else.'

'But I don't — '

'And please don't insult my intelligence by pretending not to know what I mean.' She took a deep breath, steadying herself. 'No. No, I'm sorry. I'm doing it again, aren't I? Let's make a pact: no more provocative remarks from either of us for the rest of the afternoon.'

'Suits me.' He gave his characteristic shrug and consulted his race book, controlling his emotions more quickly than she did. 'What do you fancy in the first? The runners are already leaving the mounting yard so we'll have to be quick.'

'I dunno. Like the look of that grey.'

'That's not very scientific, is it?' He looked down the list. 'And it's a filly racing against the boys.' He started to criticize her choice, only to flinch as she scowled at him. 'OK, The grey it is. I'll put it on for you. You won't get there in time if you have to run up the steps in those shoes. Fiver each way, OK?'

'No. Put ten on the nose.'

Tears started in her eyes as she watched him charge across the lawn and gallop up the steps to the tote, taking two at a time. How could someone who appeared to be so considerate, so caring, still be capable of such treachery?

He was back before the start of the race, smiling and slightly breathless. 'There you go.' He presented her with a ticket. 'Ten dollars to win on Moonsilver Princess.'

She offered him her ten dollars and he started to wave it away. 'No, you have to take it,' she said. 'Or it's bad luck.'

'OK.' He accepted it with a wry smile. 'All these racing superstitions. You're beginning to sound like your mother.'

Seconds later, the starter gave the signal and the horses were off, Moonsilver Princess left several lengths behind at the tail of the field. Foxie glanced at Daniel, daring him to say anything but he didn't. It wasn't a long race and the runners quickly reached the home turn, the race-caller clearly relishing the fact that Happy Harry, the favourite, had taken the lead and looked set to win, galloping up the straight.

'But here comes Moonsilver Princess, closing on Happy Harry fast.' The caller's voice was rising in excitement as the winning post loomed. 'Happy Harry fighting back, increasing his speed to keep the lead. They hit the line together and the judge calls for a photo but I'd say that it's Number Three, Happy Harry, just holding her off.'

'What a shame,' Daniel said. 'Should have put a fiver each way like I said. She's at good odds, too.'

But when the result of the photo was shown on the screen at the back of the course, it could be seen that Moonsilver Princess had come in first by a nose, returning Foxie $200 for her small investment of ten.

'Come on,' she laughed, after she had collected her money. 'Let's go and find our mothers and celebrate with champagne. Jim and Kerry deserve some as well.'

For a while, their differences seemed to be set aside and they were all friends together as if no trouble had come between them at all, Rose and Marion, Jim and Kerry, Foxie and Daniel, all happily celebrating the little grey filly's win.

The rest of the afternoon flew. Foxie and Daniel mingled in all the celebrity tents until it was time for the running of the celebrated Melbourne Cup.

There was a large field of twenty-four runners, including two from Ireland again and two from the UK. One of the Irish entrants, Shamrock's Fortune, was favoured to win although, with a few exceptions, the race was usually won by a local horse.

The jockeys lined up to be introduced to the crowd, some of the old hands looking bored and taking it all in their stride while the younger riders, some having a mount in the Cup for the first time, were folding their arms to stop themselves shaking or impatiently tapping their whips on their boots.

All eyes were on the entrants as they moved out on to the course, twenty-four runners, only one of which could come home a winner. There was excitement in the stands as people queued to back last-minute choices and then jostled through the crowds to find the best place to watch the race, some having to make do with the television screens scattered throughout the bars and lounges.

Foxie had used some of the money she had made earlier to back Shamrock's Fortune together with three other horses that she hoped might place. She would score a nice trifecta if it came in.

And they were off. All eyes were concentrated on the field of runners who had spread out and seemed to be taking it easy in the early part of the race. Apart from one or two parties of girls, hats askew, laughing helplessly and red-faced from sunburn and having too much to drink, the attention of everyone else on course was concentrated on the great race, the crowd subdued for the first time that day. It was a long race and seemed to take forever until the field bunched, increasing speed as the leaders reached the home turn. As they did so and Shamrock's Fortune burst through to take the lead, the roar of the crowd reached such a deafening crescendo that the race caller's voice could only just be heard.

'And the Irish stayer, Shamrock's Fortune, is out in front by four lengths — no one can touch him now.'

The rest of the field thundered past the post in a blur of colour, making it impossible to tell who were the place-getters until the photographs came in. Daniel sighed and tore up his tickets to make confetti while Foxie waited to see the numbers go up.

'Yes! Yes!' She did a little dance for joy as she saw them. 'My trifecta came in and at fairly good odds, considering the favourite won.'

After the running of the Cup and subsequent celebrations, the rest of the afternoon looked like being something of an anti-climax and the crowds started to drift away from the course. The visiting celebrities who had little interest in racing, having spent most of their time in the tents, had already gone. Rose and Marion, shoes in hand, were looking for Jim and Kerry to see if they were ready to go home. Daniel took Foxie by the arm and drew her aside.

'I don't suppose you'd like to stay and have dinner with me?'

'You suppose right,' she broke in quickly. 'Today was something of a truce behind the lines — the only way for us to get through it, really. Don't expect me to feel any happier about what you've done.'

'Foxie, for God's sake,' he blazed at her. 'What *have* I done? I'm not even sure I know what it is.'

'Liar!' she shouted back at him as her temper flared. Without thinking, she picked up a half empty glass of champagne from a nearby table and threw the dregs in his face.

For a moment, it seemed as if Daniel wouldn't react. Calmly, he took a handkerchief from his pocket, wiped his face and carefully mopped the few drops that had landed on his suit. Then quite deliberately he went back to the table, picked up a stubby someone had left almost full and poured the lot over Foxie's head, making her shriek.

'Brilliant!' A familiar voice made them stop in a frozen tableau, staring at each other. 'Thanks, you guys. Thank you for making my day.'

Angry and aware of no one but themselves, they had entirely missed the approach of Clare Mallis who was now gloating over her latest scoop.

'I hope you got all that, Toby?' She nudged her photographer who nodded, eyes sparkling as he took an additional shot of Foxie with her dress showing a wet T-shirt effect and beer still dripping from her hair. 'The editor's going to love me for this one. What shall we call it? Trouble in Paradise? Marlowe and Morgan Mayhem?' Still laughing, she moved off, leaving them both staring after her with nothing left to say.

'That was *your* fault!' They both said in unison, glaring at each other until the ridiculousness of the situation hit them both at the same time and they started to laugh.

'Foxie, you idiot,' he said when he could stop laughing enough to catch his breath. 'You've been doing this ever since we were kids. Always starting something you can't finish. Never learned to control your temper, have you?'

'Excuse me!' she fired up, ready to go for him all over again. 'I'm not the only one with red hair and a temper to match.'

'Ssh!' he said, glancing around. 'Don't make such a noise. You'll bring Clare Mallis back.'

'She's already done her worst. What more can she do?'

'I dread to think. She'll be back with a movie camera next. Look, Foxie, all joking apart, you should come back to my place and dry off. You can't possibly drive home in wet clothes.'

'I don't care. I'd rather catch my death of cold than sup with the devil.'

'How medieval.' He shrugged, shaking his head. 'But suit yourself.'

'Thank you, I will.' She knew she sounded less than gracious, but she knew what a sight she looked with limp feathers dripping off her head and a dress that was now clinging to her and smelling like a brewery. It didn't help to know she had no one to blame but herself. She was tired, dispirited and all she wanted now was to get home and call an end to what had ultimately been a trying day.

But even when she reached the safe haven of her car, it took a very long time to get away from the course. Opportunistic policemen had brought a booze bus to the main exit and were stopping every car before it could leave. Frantically, Foxie cast her mind back to the champagne she had drunk so carelessly that morning, grateful that she'd been too busy to drink anything but water since.

All the same, her clothes reeked of alcohol and the young policeman gave her a piercing look as he thrust the breathalizer towards her to test the level of alcohol on her breath. She tried to look nonchalant as she awaited the result, thinking how inconvenient as well as shaming it would be to lose her driver's licence today.

Looking almost disappointed when he found a negative result, the policeman waved her on, preparing to accost the next driver.

⋆ ⋆ ⋆

No peace awaited her at home, either. She had been looking forward to soaking in a hot bath, then getting into a nightie and dressing-gown before making herself a light supper to take to bed. Instead, Marion burst from the house and came running towards the car even before she could turn off the engine.

'Oh, Foxie. I've been trying to ring you but your mobile seems to be off. Thank goodness you're home.'

'What's happened now, Mum?' she asked with a sinking heart.

'Down at the stables — Dangerous Red.'

'Oh God, he's not sick, is he? What happened? He's supposed to be racing on Thursday.'

'Well, I don't know about that. Jim's walking him now. He said for you to get down there soon as you came home.'

'Has he sent for the vet?'

'I don't know. I don't think so. He was waiting to see what you thought.'

'Good Lord, Mum. Does everyone wait for me to do everything around here?'

'Now I know it's annoying but don't go taking your temper out on Jim. He feels guilty enough already for being away when it happened.'

Foxie took a deep breath, kicked off her sandals in the porch and put on her wellingtons. She snatched a short jacket from behind the door and pulled it on over the silk chiffon dress, which was probably ruined anyway, then headed out to the stables.

'Jim?' she called as soon as she got there. 'How sick is he? Is he lying down?'

'He wants to but I've been walking him to make sure he doesn't.' Jim stuck his head out from the stall. 'I'm afraid it might be colic. If not, it's a spider bite.'

'A spider bite?' Foxie shuddered and started glancing around apprehensively. 'What sort of spider?'

'White-tail probably. They love timber and get everywhere. I've never seen it but I've heard horses can die of the pain from a spider bite.'

'Don't even think of it. Have you sent for the vet?'

'Not yet, but I'm thinkin' we should. Although where we're to get one who's half sober on Melbourne Cup night I've no idea.'

Once more Red tried to lie down and roll before Jim got him up again, making him walk.

'Not comfortable, is he?' Foxie said.

'Far from it. But there's no sign of lameness,' Jim said. 'My guess is colic.'

'Poor old fellow.' Foxie patted the horse's neck. 'No racing for you on Thursday, then.'

'Or for some time, if it is.'

'Who do we usually call? Old Sampson?'

'I suppose. He was always reliable in your father's day.' Jim shook his head. 'But nowadays all you get is a locum because the old man's never there. Spends most of his time up in Port Douglas with his popsy — '

Foxie couldn't help giggling at the old-fashioned expression.

'Ain't no laughin' matter, Foxie. Some o'

those locums are good an' some are just small animal vets who wouldn't know one end of a horse from another.'

'Oh dear.' Foxie headed for the phone in the office. 'Well, I suppose I'd better ring Sampson's and see who's there.'

No one answered her call at the surgery until it was picked up by a very old tape in an answering machine, inviting her to leave a message for someone to contact her the following day.

'I don't want someone tomorrow!' she yelled at it in frustration. 'We need help now. Where's the yellow pages?' She started rummaging for the directory in the desk until she realized Jim was standing beside her.

'There's always Mr Morgan,' he suggested. 'He used to be a vet.'

'Exactly. Used to be. Even if he knows what to do for Red, he won't have any supplies.'

'Still got his ticket, hasn't he? He can get some.'

Foxie thought about it, still reluctant to call Daniel who would have made other plans for the evening by now. In the end she decided that her pride was far less important than treatment for Dangerous Red, so she made the call.

She was taken aback when his telephone was answered by a girl with a strong Irish accent. He hadn't wasted much time in replacing her with a date for this evening.

'Hello? This is Daniel Morgan's phone.'

'Is Daniel there?' she said more sharply than she intended.

'Yes. And if you're his girlfriend, please don't get yourself in a state because I'm only — '

'Laura! Who is it?' She heard Daniel in the background, getting ready to take the phone.

'Some girl. She seems a bit put out. I was tryin' to tell her that I'm not your girlfriend.'

She heard Daniel groan and take the phone from her. 'Morgan here. Who is this?'

'Daniel, it's Foxie.'

'Well, well.' He didn't sound all that pleased to hear from her. 'After that scene at the races, I thought I'd heard the last of you for today.'

'I'm sure. Since you've invited along that breathless little Irish person who isn't your girlfriend.'

'You mean Laura?' He chuckled. 'She's just a cousin.'

'Really? I never met any cousin of yours before.'

'You wouldn't have had the chance. She's only just over from Ireland and green as the Emerald Isle itself. Really Foxie, unless this call is important, we were just on our way out

260

to dinner. We're starving.'

'Well, you might have to starve a bit longer. I'm sorry, Daniel, but when Jim got back to the stables, he found Red was really quite sick. He thinks it's colic.'

'How serious is it? Have you called the vet?'

'Our usual man can't be contacted. So Jim thought of you.'

'OK. I'll see if I can get hold of supplies and be there as soon as I can.'

'I'm sorry, Daniel.'

'For what? Ruining my evening?'

'That, too. And you'd better bring Laura with you; you can't leave her in town on her own.'

'Thanks. I will. Should be with you in an hour or so, depending how long it takes me to stock my bag.'

★ ★ ★

While they were waiting for Daniel to arrive, Foxie ran upstairs to change out of her ruined dress. She removed the stale makeup she had been wearing all day and took a quick shower, washing her hair which still smelled of beer. Feeling better, she dressed quickly in jeans and a long-sleeved sweatshirt before putting some moisturiser on her pink, slightly sunburned face. Divested of the remains of her earlier glamour, she went downstairs to help Marion and Rose with the evening meal.

While Marion prepared a nourishing, chunky vegetable soup to feed everyone, Rose made delicious wholemeal bread although they knew no one would feel like eating anything until they were sure Red was safe.

Daniel arrived just before eight o'clock, having changed from his suit into jeans and a polo neck under a light blue sweater. Somehow the casual clothes softened his appearance, making his features less preda-tory. He came into the kitchen via the back door, his diminutive Irish cousin hanging back shyly behind him.

It was Rose who held out her arms to the girl, greeting her with a hug. 'You must be Laura. I've heard so many nice things about you. I met your mother when I went to Europe — oh, so many years ago now — we were always the best of friends. You look just as she did at your age.'

'Everyone says that. An' Mum never stops talkin' about you, neither.' Laura glanced around the room, ready to meet everyone else until she saw Foxie, when she gasped and stood wide-eyed, hands flying to her mouth. 'But I know you, don't I? You're Carole Parker!'

'Not any more,' Foxie smiled, holding out her hand. 'I'm Jane Marlowe but mostly my friends call me Foxie.'

'Foxie, it is then. An' you're even prettier than you look on TV,' the girl enthused. 'I used to watch *The Brave and the Free* every day when I came home from school.'

'Did you now?' Foxie raised her eyebrows, not at all sure that this was a compliment.

'All that red hair an' your white streak. So unusual. I remember thinkin' it had to be a wig.'

'As you see, it isn't.' Foxie felt slightly impatient, having had conversations like this before. 'Look, can you do some catching up with Rose and my mother while I take Daniel across to the stables?'

'Gosh, yes. I'm sorry.' The girl looked abashed. 'I was forgetting about the poor horse. I hope he'll be OK.'

★   ★   ★

At the stables, Jim was still waiting impatiently, concerned about the horse. Quickly, he gave Daniel a run-down on his condition. He had grown suspicious as soon as he came home and found the horse sweating and restless, wanting to lie down.

'An' I wish I hadn't gone to the races now,'

he concluded, shaking his head. 'Then this wouldn't have happened.'

'You can't be here all the time, Jim,' Foxie said gently. 'It might've happened anyway.'

With gentle hands, Daniel examined the horse all over and in particular listened to his gut.

'Hopefully, it's not serious,' he said at last. 'And I don't think there's a twist. We'll give him some painkillers and anti-inflammatories and keep an eye on him to see how he does.' He opened his bag and prepared several injections which he quickly gave to the horse.

'That's it for now,' he said. 'But he won't be racing again for quite a while. And somebody ought to stay up with him tonight to make sure he's OK.'

'I will,' Jim said, although he was stifling a yawn.

'No, Jim, you look all in,' Foxie said. 'And you have to be up with everyone else in the morning. I'll do it.'

'Then I'll sit up with you,' Daniel said.

'There's really no need,' she started to say, till he cut her protests short.

'And what will you do if he takes a turn for the worse? You'll only have to call me again.'

'OK then.' She gave in with bad grace.

12

Back at the house, they made short work of Marion's vegetable stew, anxious to get back to the horse. Laura entertained them with tales of her travels across Europe and various scrapes, although Foxie couldn't help feeling that either the Irish girl was putting on an act or she was unusually naïve. After their day at the races and cooking for everyone at the end of it, Marion and Rose were exhausted and ready for bed and book. Before retiring, Rose made up the spare bed in her room for Laura, leaving the girl downstairs to watch an old film on TV.

On the way to the stables again, accompanied by Witherspoon, the old greyhound who would still rather spend his time in the stables than up at the house, Foxie made one last attempt to get Daniel to leave. She couldn't help thinking of the awkward conversations that might take place during the course of a long night.

'Look, I have Witherspoon for company and really, if we find the horse more settled and out of danger, there's no need for two people to lose a night's sleep over it.'

He stopped dead in his tracks to look at her. 'Foxie, I know it would be more convenient for you if I were to leave. To be honest, it would suit me, too. But I'm not going. Dangerous Red is far too important to all of us. He's the first horse we've had who looks like coming through as a champion and we owe it to Barry as much as ourselves, to give him the very best care that we can. I'm taking no chances.'

She stared at him, thinking once again that this was a side of Daniel that didn't match up to the ruthless businessman she knew him to be.

'I forgot all about Barry,' she groaned. 'He'll be so disappointed when I tell him we have to scratch.'

'I'll do it. He doesn't like hearing bad news and can be a bit of a bully sometimes.'

Inside the stables, Jim cautiously reported a change for the better.

'We're in luck. Looks like we caught it in time. He's stopped nipping himself and seems much calmer now. I think he'll settle for the night. An' if it's all the same to you, I'll turn in myself.' He stifled a yawn. 'By the way, I found out how it happened. It was Sharon, the new girl. Thought she was bein' helpful and accidentally changed his feed.'

'Without asking permission?' Daniel fired

266

up at once. 'She could've killed him. I hope you told her how serious it is.'

'Matter of fact, I didn't.' Jim shrugged, looking uncomfortable. 'Poor girl feels badly enough as it is.'

'Then I'll speak to her myself in the morning.'

'I wish you wouldn't do that, Mr Morgan.' As always when he felt at a disadvantage, Jim used formal address. 'Sharon's a good worker and it was a genuine mistake. I'm sure she's learned her lesson and won't let it happen again.'

'I rely on you to see that she doesn't. Because of her bad decision, the horse may not race for some time. That means loss of revenue for the stables as well as the owners.'

'No one knows that better'n I do, sir. An' if there's nothin' else, I'll bid you goodnight.' Jim gave Foxie a wry salute. 'Miss Marlowe.'

'Goodnight, Jim, and thanks for everything.' She gave him her brightest smile, trying to make up for Daniel's criticism.

'Jim has to have a break some time,' she rebuked him gently when the stable foreman was out of earshot. 'He won't feel the same about Melbourne Cup Day after this.'

'I know. It's just that we're not out of the woods yet. And I'm not really an expert. Perhaps I should get a second opinion just to confirm it isn't a twisted bowel.'

'Not unless he takes a turn for the worse.'

Hearing this, Daniel examined the animal all over again but, much as he expected, it was too soon to see any change. Satisfied that there was no more he could do for the horse, he looked around for a means to make them comfortable for their long vigil and pulled down several bales of fresh straw to contrive a makeshift couch. While he tested it by flinging himself down and stretching out full-length, Foxie perched on the edge, still feeling awkward and ambivalent about her feelings for Daniel, wondering how they would get through what promised to be a long night. Seeing how ill at ease she was, Daniel laughed.

'Foxie, relax,' he said. 'You look tense as Bluebeard's latest bride, sitting there waiting for the old fellow to pounce.'

She laughed, feeling silly because she had been thinking something along those lines. 'There are some magazines in Jim's office,' she offered. 'Would you like me to bring you . . .?'

He shook his head. 'No, thanks. I don't suppose Jim's taste is the same as mine.'

'Scrabble? Monopoly? We have them up at the house.'

'Ugh,' he pulled a face. 'You know I hate board games.'

'Right.' She sat on her hands, relapsing into a silence that seemed to go on forever, unanswered queries hanging heavy in the air between them.

'Daniel,' she said at last, unable to bear it any longer. 'If I ask you something important, will you answer me honestly?'

'Oh, here we go,' he murmured, rolling his eyes to heaven. 'I hope this isn't going to turn into the night of the grand inquisition.'

'You wanted to stay so you can't blame me for taking advantage. I've been wondering why you paid back the money I spent on Dangerous Red? Does this mean we're not partners any more?'

'Good Lord, no.' He stared at her, shocked. 'I never expected you to think that.'

'Then why did you do it?'

'I'd have thought that was obvious.'

'Not to me.'

'After I sold the fitness centre, I did it as an act of good faith. You seemed to think I was trying to cheat you and I thought if I gave back your investment, you'd think well of me. I was wrong, of course.'

'Why should you care what I think when you're breaking the partnership anyway by selling us out to Boulter Brothers? Mum no longer cares, she's going to Queensland. But I feel as if I'm sitting here, waiting for the axe to fall. I know it's only a question of time.'

'Foxie, listen to me and listen good.' He spoke slowly and deliberately. 'I have no intention of selling these stables to Boulter Brothers.'

Her voice rose. 'But I talked to Doug Boulter myself.'

'Yes. And I wish you hadn't.'

'I'm sure you do!'

'Keep your voice down, Foxie, you're disturbing the horse.'

'If there's one thing I can't stand, it's lies,' she hissed at him.

'And if there's one thing *I* can't stand,' he murmured through gritted teeth, glaring as if he would like to strangle her, 'it's a stubborn woman who'll believe the worst of a man without giving him a chance to explain.'

'All right then, explain. I'm all ears. We have the whole night ahead of us, after all.'

'All right, I will. But before that, to keep things even, I have one or two questions of my own. What exactly was your American friend doing here besides stealing my PA? My mother thought he was trying to tempt you to go back to the show.'

'He was. But I turned him down.' She laughed shortly. 'The nerve of the man. Wanted me to check into a health farm and lose three kilos.'

'Really? And that was your only reason for turning your back on lots of money and a shiny new contract? When our mothers were already committed to a new life in Queensland and you thought I was selling the stables from under you? No Foxie, I don't buy it. You'll have to do better than that.'

'It's true. He said I must lose three kilos at least and put extensions in my hair until it grew long again.'

'Come on Foxie, these are just details. There has to be something more.'

'All right, there was. But I'm not sure I want to tell you. You'll only laugh.'

He raised two fingers in a solemn salute. 'I promise I won't. Scout's honour.'

'Daniel, you were never a boy scout.'

'No but it sounds good, doesn't it? So tell me? What did Creepy Carstairs want you to do that was so terrible? My imagination's running riot.'

'It was nothing like that. And he's not creepy; he comes right out and says what he wants. Fortunately, he doesn't take offence when girls turn him down.' She gave him a quick glance and saw his lips twitching. 'You *are* going to laugh. I don't want to tell you now.'

'Oh yes, you will,' he said, pinching her waist and making her squirm and give a stifled shriek. 'You expect me to put all my cards on the table.'

'All right then. He wanted to resurrect Carole Parker.' She hesitated, hoping that would be enough.

'Oh, I never saw that one coming,' he said sarcastically. 'And?'

Foxie took a deep breath. 'And he wanted to introduce Pepper Harcourt as Carole's long-lost Australian daughter.'

Daniel let out a bark of delighted laughter, making Foxie react by giving him a slap on the back of the head.

'Hey!' He stopped laughing at once, rubbing it. 'You pack a wallop, Foxie. I only laughed because you're not old enough to play the mother of a 19-year-old girl.'

'They don't seem to care about small details like that.'

He considered this news for a moment and brightened, struck by a new thought. 'So what's going to happen to Pepper if you back out? Will he send her home?'

'I don't think so. He's so pleased with his latest Australian acquisition, he's working up several alternative storylines. That way they're never left without something to shoot.'

'Poor old Pep. Lets hope it turns out to be the rainbow's end she thinks it will be.'

'It will. I had the best time ever in LA at

her age. And, whatever you think of Cam, he's good at his job. If he really puts his mind to it, he can make her a star.'

'He certainly made a star out of you. I've never seen so many people thrilled to meet Carole Parker at the races today.'

'And some not so thrilled.' Foxie's smiled faded, remembering Stella.

'Don't even think of that woman. She's the exception that proves the rule.'

'Do you want some coffee?' she said, changing the subject. She didn't want to talk about Stella. 'Jim has a drip-filter machine in the office.'

'Might be a good way of keeping awake.'

Grateful to have something to do, Foxie brewed coffee, taking as long as she could. Eventually, she had to return carrying two steaming mugs and a plate of chocolate Tim Tams. 'I hope you still take milk and two sugars?'

He nodded, accepting it, his eyes lighting up when he saw the chocolate biscuits. 'My favourite. You remembered.'

'Jim's favourite too — and Witherspoon's.' She tossed one to the dog who crunched it with relish.

'Chocolate is bad for dogs,' Daniel grumbled.

She ignored the remark and looked across

at the horse, sipping her coffee and nibbling a biscuit. 'Red seems a lot more comfortable than he was.'

'Yes. Hopefully, it was only a mild attack.' He glanced at his watch. 'Look, Foxie, there's really no need for you to miss a night's rest. I'm quite happy to stay up with the horse on my own.'

'Great. Now you've had your Tim Tams, you want to get rid of me,' she teased. 'I don't think so. Now I've satisfied your curiosity, I'm going to sit here until you've satisfied mine.'

'Fire away, then.' He shrugged, resigned to it. 'What is it you want to know?'

'Lots of things. To begin with, anyone can see you love animals. You're a good judge of horseflesh and you've been marvellous tonight here with Red. So, after going through all that trouble to get qualified, why did you give up being a full-time vet?'

'It wasn't an easy decision. For the whole of my childhood, I'd thought of nothing else — being nothing else. I sailed through the theory of veterinary medicine but when it came to practical matters, I hit the wall. To gain experience, I had to join a busy teaching practice as a junior vet. The very first day I was there, I had too many hard decisions to take. I'd set out to become a healer of animals, not a mercy killer. I hated to see old people weeping as they left behind pets that had been their companions for years. Sometimes we had to kill healthy animals too, simply because they weren't wanted; it was impossible to find homes for all of them. I had studied for years to get where I was, only to find it was not what I wanted at all.'

'I can understand that,' she said. 'Everyone thinks it would be wonderful to be a vet, and most of the time it is. But nobody likes to think of the darker side. What happened after that?'

He shrugged. 'I used a small legacy from an uncle in Ireland to take a business course. Then I found I could make money by working up ailing businesses and selling them again at a profit. From there on, I've never looked back.'

'And have you always sold every business you've owned?'

'So far, I suppose so.' He thought for a moment. 'Yes.'

'And you still want me to believe you won't sell the stables to Boulter Brothers?'

'OK. For you to understand the whole story, we'll have to go back to a time several months before you came home. And I'm warning you now, you're not going to like some of this.'

'Go on.'

'Your father knew he had inoperable cancer and was hoping for a quick end to his suffering. Instead he lived on, dying by inches. Marion tried to cope but John had been her anchor all of her life and she couldn't. She just fell apart.'

'Why didn't anyone tell me? I would have come home before.'

'She kept saying she wanted to go it alone, that you had your own life to lead and she didn't want you upset.'

'That makes me feel ten times worse about it now.'

'I did say there were some things you wouldn't like to hear.'

'It's all right. Go on.'

'Through the grapevine, Doug Boulter heard that your father was steadily losing business and the stables were in trouble and he saw an opportunity for himself.'

She waved her hand impatiently. 'Daniel, this is stale news. I've heard it already.'

'But what you don't know is that right after your father died, he kept calling your mother at home almost daily, urging her to sell. And not in a pleasant way, either. He told her that each week she postponed her decision, he would reduce his offer by several thousand dollars.'

'No, I didn't know that,' Foxie whispered.

'And she never said.'

'That's when my mother asked me to intervene. She was afraid Marion was on the verge of suicide and couldn't take any more. It wasn't a good time for me, either. I was financially stretched, having just taken on the fitness centre, but I thought if I could rescue Marlowe's and turn it into a viable business again, I might deal with Boulters myself and stop them harassing your mother. But when I took over and looked into your father's financial affairs, I found the trouble was even deeper than I thought. I had no choice but to think of selling again even if I had to take a loss.'

'So it's true, isn't it? You *are* dealing with Boulter Brothers?'

'For the last time — no! And certainly not after you came home and agreed to go into partnership over the syndication idea.'

'But Doug Boulter told me he had contracts ready for you to sign.'

'I know. That's how he operates. Drawing up contracts before discussions have scarcely begun and then browbeating people into signing them. And, if that doesn't work, he calls up the stables to spread doubt and confusion among the workers, make them worry about losing their jobs. He probably knew very well he was talking to John

Marlowe's daughter. There won't be too many grooms here with American accents. It's much more pronounced on the phone.'

'And I fell for it, didn't I?'

'Why not? It isn't easy to get the best of that old snake in the grass.'

'So it was all a scam? You're not thinking of signing any contracts with Boulters?'

'Foxie, with my hand on my heart the only contract I've already signed is the one Harvey Watson is holding for you.'

'Ohh.' She groaned, biting her lip. 'And I told Miss Beech to tear it up.'

'Miss Beech is too sensible to do anything so impulsive. In any case I've already spoken to Harvey myself and explained the situation. He quite understands.'

'Then why didn't anyone take the time to explain it to me?'

He looked at her and she realized he was laughing softly. 'Have you any idea how hard it is to talk to you when you're filled with righteous indignation?'

'You could have tried.'

'I did. Many times.'

'I suppose you think I owe you an apology now?'

'No. I'm sure you hate eating humble pie just as much as I do. Just don't be so ready to think the worst of me, that's all.'

'I won't,' she whispered, leaning her forehead against his shoulder. 'Daniel, I'm so sorry.'

He took advantage of her nearness to pull her into his embrace. He kissed her slowly but thoroughly, giving her no chance to pull away. Tense to begin with, slowly she relaxed against him, revelling in the smell of new wool, combined with his subtle but expensive aftershave, allowing him to press her into the accommodating straw of their makeshift couch.

He pushed up her sweater, delighted to find that she was wearing no bra and pressed his lips to first one breast and then the other, teasing the nipples until they peaked, growing hard as berries in his mouth. Almost purring with the sensuous pleasure of it all, she drew him closer, at the same time pushing her thigh against him to feel his arousal.

'Oh, Foxie,' he sighed. 'What are you doing to me?'

She gave a low gurgle of laughter before drawing him back to her mouth to kiss him again. But instead of continuing the lovemaking to its natural conclusion, he ended the kiss and pulled down her sweater before rearranging his own clothes. 'Not now,' he whispered. 'This isn't the time or the place.'

'What are you saying?' Her heart felt as if it

had turned in her chest. 'You've gone off me? You don't want me any more?'

'No. Why must you always misunderstand? Someone might come in here in here at any moment and catch us in the act. This is a public place.'

'Nobody's going to come here at this time of night. And even if they did, I'm sure they'd be discreet enough to turn right around and go out.'

As if on cue, a timid voice called softly from the open front door while Witherspoon got up and went to see who it was.

'Foxie? Daniel? Are you in there?'

'Laura,' Daniel mouthed, quickly picking tell-tale pieces of straw out of Foxie's hair and brushing them off her back. Then he stood up and leaned over the door of the stall, beckoning the girl to come in and join them. 'We're down here, Laura. What's up?'

'Nothin'. I came to see how the horse was doing, that's all. An' it's too quiet up there at the house. Everyone's gone to bed and there's nothing on the TV, so I thought you might like some company.' No stranger to a scuffle in the dark herself, she knew exactly what they had been doing when she saw their flushed faces and ill-concealed breathlessness. 'But I guess not.' Then she added in a stage whisper to Daniel. 'Did she say *yes*?'

'Shut up, Laura! I haven't asked her yet.'

'Asked me what?' Foxie had long ears.

Daniel took a deep breath. 'All right. Foxie, I'm not asking any more, I'm telling you — we're getting married.'

'Oh are we?' She fired up at once. 'This is a bit sudden, isn't it?'

'Not really.' He forged on, warming to the idea now he had started. 'I've tried to make occasions to propose to you nicely with flowers and dinners by candlelight but somehow it never worked out. So you'll have to put up with sawdust and straw. I love you Foxie and you love me — you know you do. You just don't want to admit it, that's all.'

'Oh, that's so beautiful,' Laura sighed. 'How could any girl resist that?'

'Very easily.' Foxie narrowed her eyes and sat there, folding her arms. 'I can't deny there's a certain chemistry between us, Daniel, but we always end up fighting like cat and dog. It happened again at the races today. Why on earth should I want to get married to you?'

'Because nobody else will put up with either of us and I want the matter settled, once and for all.'

'Then I'll put you out of your misery and settle it now. I have no intention of getting married right now — to you or to anyone else.'

'Ohh!' Laura groaned. 'And I did so want to be a bridesmaid.'

'Bridesmaid?' Foxie glanced at her nervously. 'This is moving way too fast for me.'

'Not fast enough.' Daniel hugged her possessively. 'Time is passing, my love. Think of your biological clock, ticking away towards thirty, tick-tock!'

'Stop that at once.' She pulled free. 'I'm not even sure I want kids. Red-faced, screaming babies, filthy nappies and sleepless nights.'

'Look on the bright side,' said Laura. 'They'll grow up and take care of you in your old age.'

'I can take care of my own old age.' Foxie scowled.

'But wouldn't you rather spend it with me?' Daniel tried a different tack. 'Two old grey heads in rocking chairs, sitting before the fire?'

Foxie's scowl deepened.

'I'm not helpin',' am I?' Laura looked anxious. 'Maybe you'll do better on your own. G'night, Cous.' She paused to give Daniel a kiss on the cheek and smiled at Foxie, adding in a stage whisper. 'Maybe she'll change her mind when she sees the ring.' And with a mischievous laugh she left the stall, running towards the open stable door.

282

'What ring?' Foxie had sharp ears.

There was no time for Daniel to answer her because there was a small shriek from Laura, bringing Daniel to his feet muttering 'What the hell?'

Two men loomed in the doorway, marching Laura between them. She looked scared.

'This place isn't very secure.' The older man grinned, pushing an old-fashioned fedora to the back of his head. 'Boss isn't going to like that. Anyone could walk in off the street just as we did.'

'We're not open for visitors,' Daniel said, patting his pockets in the hope of finding his mobile until he realized he had left it on the kitchen table in the house. 'You do know you're trespassing on private property and — '

'Put a sock in it,' the man said. 'Just do as we say and the ladies won't have to get hurt.' He opened a briefcase and took out some documents. 'The boss says he's tired of waitin'. Sent us with these contracts he wants you to sign.'

'Did he now. How did you know where to find me?'

'You should be more careful what you leave on your answerin' machine. 'Anyone needs me, I'll be at Marlowe's till tomorrow', you said, 'sittin' up with a sick horse'.' The man gave Red a slap on the rump, making him kick out. 'He don't look all that sick to me.'

'Well, you've had a wasted journey,' Daniel said. 'And you can take those contracts right back where they came from. A document isn't legal if it's signed under duress.' He paused, flinching, as Laura cried out in pain. The larger man had hold of her hand and was squeezing it.

'Oh, dear. Now that's not very nice is it, Kev.' The older man turned towards his companion who was grinning unpleasantly, enjoying the prospect of hurting Laura. 'Bending the young lady's finger like that. Shame if you had to break it.'

'All right,' Daniel muttered. 'Give the damned papers. I'll sign.' But at the same time he managed to give Foxie a surreptitious wink.

After that, two things happened in quick succession. At a hidden signal from Foxie and without troubling to announce himself with a bark, Witherspoon hurled himself at the man holding Laura and fastened his teeth in his muscular thigh. Howling in pain, Kevin let go of her, turning his attention to the dog, intending to break his neck. Before he could so, Foxie swung a heavy metal bucket, clouting the man on the side of the head. It was a lucky blow, striking the temple, and he collapsed, felled like an ox. For a moment she stared at him, wide-eyed, hoping she hadn't killed him.

At the same time all this was going on, Daniel threw himself at the older man in a rugby tackle, to bring him crashing to the ground.

'Kevin! Do something, you mug,' the man yelled, not realizing that his brutish sidekick was in no position to help him.

The horse, who had been standing quietly up until now, suddenly panicked and reared. He would have brought his hooves crashing down on both Daniel and the intruder, if Foxie hadn't the presence of mind to take hold of his leading rein and pull him aside.

'Poor fellow. Poor Red,' She whispered, rubbing his nose to comfort the horse who was upset and shivering with fright. 'It's OK now.'

Laura, recovering quickly, found a rope and helped Daniel to tie the two men together in the passage outside the stalls. For a sick horse, Dangerous Red had had more than enough excitement for one night.

'All right you, I want some answers.' Daniel prodded the smaller man with his foot, making him flinch. Kevin, groaning as he began to come round, tried to sit up and vomited all over his own clothes.

His companion grimaced at the smell.

'That's disgusting. Can't you hose him down?'

'Later,' Daniel snapped. 'I don't like thugs who hurt girls. Firstly, how did you get here?'

'Boss sent us down in a hired car,' the man said. 'He's waitin' for us back at the hotel in town.'

'Doug Boulter is here? In Melbourne? Staying where?'

The man looked even more apprehensive. 'He's not goin' to like it if we tell you.'

'Where?' Daniel said through gritted teeth, prodding him once again with his booted foot.

'All right.' The man gasped, fearing a kicking. 'The Meridian. Room four twenty-four. But he's flyin' out first thing in the morning.'

'I don't think so. Not without these.' He went back to Red's stall and picked up what remained of the contracts, ruined now, having been trampled by the horse. 'I think I'll be paying a visit to Mr Boulter. Soon as I've handed you over to the police.'

'You wouldn't do that!'

'And I shall be pressing charges as well. You have trespassed on private property, assaulted my cousin and threatened the life of a valuable horse. That's quite enough for them to hold you.'

'Kev wouldn't have hurt her, not really.' The man started to whine. 'An' look what she done to 'im.' The man jerked his head towards Foxie. 'Proper bloody amazon, ain't she?'

'Yes,' Daniel smiled ruefully. 'I'm afraid she is. But you are intruders and we can prove it was self-defence.'

'The door was open, wasn't it? We didn't break in. Can't we settle this amicable, jus' between ourselves? No need to stir up the coppers, is there?'

'There's been nothing friendly about any of this. I'm calling the police and charges will be laid. Hopefully, you'll go to jail and your shady-looking boss along with you.'

While Daniel and Laura went to the office to report the matter to the police, Foxie walked Red who seemed a lot stronger and no longer in danger of collapse.

Jim and his lads arrived at the stables at dawn, surprised to find a police car outside and officers arresting and handcuffing the two men.

'That's it, lads. The excitement's over,' Daniel said, as the police car moved slowly away. 'Back to work now. And you, Laura, had better get your head down. A couple of hours' sleep will be better than none.'

'I'm too wound up to sleep a wink,' Laura

started to say until Daniel gave her a meaningful look.

'Laura, just go,' he said softly, leading them both towards the house.

'Oh. Oh, I see. G'night for the third time, then,' the girl said.

Finding herself alone in the kitchen with Daniel, Foxie busied herself making coffee, very much aware he was hovering behind her.

'Now then,' he whispered, standing so close she could feel his warm breath on the back of her neck. 'Where were we when we were so rudely interrupted? I think we were talking about a ring.'

'Laura was.' Foxie busied herself at the Aga. 'Lucky we keep the fire in at night, all ready for bacon and eggs in the morning. Want some?'

'Later,' he said. 'Aren't you the least bit curious about this ring?'

'Nope. If I haven't seen it, I won't miss it, will I?'

'Foxie, be serious. Are you really turning me down?'

'I'm not sure you want to marry me for the right reasons.'

'Now what does that mean.' His temper was rising again. 'It sounds just stupid enough to be a piece of script-writing from that soap opera of yours.'

'Maybe it is. Lots of our stories were true to life.'

'Then let's keep it simple, shall we? I love you. You love me — '

'How do you come to that conclusion? I've never said so. And until now, you've never said it to me.'

'Sometimes words aren't necessary. Every time we kiss, I can feel that you love me, every time I hold you in my arms.'

'Daniel I've already told you, that's just chemistry, otherwise known as common or garden lust.'

'Well, it's all very enjoyable, isn't it? And lots of marriages are built on much less. We're good judges of horseflesh; we can go to New Zealand again and buy another horse like Dangerous Red. And besides that, look at our co-ordination, how we worked in sync to outwit those thugs.'

'Those idiots? We wouldn't have had to be Einstein, would we?' She pressed a mug of coffee into his hands to occupy them. 'What are we going to do about old Boulter, then?'

'Not much. I asked the police to call round and give him a fright. Long as he takes the hired help back to Sydney and we hear no more from him, that's good enough for me. No point making an implacable enemy is there?'

She smiled, shaking her head. 'You never cease to amaze me, Daniel. The way you talked to those men, I felt sure you wouldn't rest till you had them rotting in jail.'

'Like I said, I wanted to give them a fright.'

At that moment, the kitchen door burst open to admit Marion wrapped in a candlewick dressing-gown and brandishing the morning papers.

'Honestly, you two!' She flung the tabloid down on the kitchen table. 'I expected you to make me proud on Melbourne Cup Day but here you are, large as life, behaving like unruly teenagers.'

'Let's see,' Foxie grinned, catching sight of the full colour photograph of Daniel and herself, soaking wet and glaring at each other at the races. 'Daniel, look. We beat Shamrock's Fortune to the front page!'

On the following page was a smaller series of photographs showing the events leading up to Foxie's wet dress with the headline *Lovers' Tiff at the Cup.*

He leaned over her shoulder, reading Clare Mallis's spiteful words. *Would you trust your money to such irresponsible people? I don't think so. Daniel Morgan and Jane Marlowe, who won't see thirty again —*

'Hey, that's below the belt,' Foxie said. 'I'm only twenty-eight.'

Behaving like schoolies on the rampage. Drunk, disorderly and brawling outside the Emirates' Tent at the Melbourne Cup.

'For a start, we weren't drunk,' Daniel put in.

'It's a good thing I'm going to Queensland where nobody knows me. I'll never be able to hold up my head again,' Marion groaned. 'And Foxie, look at you in that soaking wet dress; you might as well be wearing nothing at all. And stop giggling, you two,' she said, as she realized Daniel and Foxie had dissolved into helpless laughter again. 'You have your reputation to think of. And that of the stables. This is no laughing matter.'

But Marion's indignant expression only made them laugh all the more.

'That's one for the scrap-book, isn't it?' Daniel said, wiping tears of mirth from his eyes.

'Scrap-book?' Marion glared at him. 'In your shoes, I should want to go out and buy as many copies as I could lay my hands on, then make a big bonfire of the lot.'

'No, Mum,' Foxie said, smiling at Daniel. 'Because we're going to make a liar out of Clare Mallis, aren't we, Daniel? We're getting married.'

'But you can't.' Instead of being delighted, as they expected, Marion looked appalled.

291

'You absolutely can't. Not now. Not yet.'

'Why ever not, Mum?' Foxie stared at her. 'Isn't this what you and Rose have been plotting and planning all along? We thought you'd be pleased.'

'Yes, it is. And we are. It's just that Rose won't believe we're putting off going to Queensland yet again.'

13

Clare Mallis answered her editor's summons to come to his office with a happy heart. Here it was at last. Her promotion, her reward for the hundreds of birthday parties, weddings and local fashion parades she had been forced to cover over the years. Now the gossip column would be a thing of the past; she was about to join the ranks of real journalists in the front line. She might even be invited to join the crew of *Sixty Minutes*, a job which would lead her into a glamorous new television career.

The expression on her editor's face banished all such illusions. It was thunderous. A man well into his sixties and approaching retirement, he suffered from intestinal cramps which tormented him more than ever when he was angry.

'Ms Mallis!' he began in low but venomous tones. 'Your inaccurate reporting is going to damage the reputation of this newspaper. You have made fools of us all!'

'In-inaccurate reporting?' she stammered, turning her head to peer at the series of pictures on the second page of today's issue, lying open in front of him. 'But I promise you, sir, that's exactly how it happened. The camera cannot lie.'

'It can and this time it did. I've just received a phone call from Daniel Morgan informing me that he and Ms Marlowe are getting hitched very shortly, and wondering if we would like to send someone to cover the wedding? He was being facetious but I accepted, of course, before he starts talking to anyone else. I also told him I knew just the person to do it.' He stabbed a finger towards her, making her blink. 'You!'

★   ★   ★

If Foxie and Daniel had been hoping for a quiet, intimate wedding with just a few family members and close friends, they were doomed to be disappointed.

Barry Glenn, having come to the stables in a fury when he heard that Dangerous Red was unfit to race on Oaks Day, was soon mollified when he saw the care and attention that had been lavished on the horse. Of course, nobody mentioned the visit of Boulter Brothers' heavies and the upset they had caused. There was no need as Dangerous Red was himself again and well on the road to recovery.

But, as soon as he got wind of the wedding about to take place, he was all set to take charge, wanting to turn it into a major media event and dismiss their original ideal of having a simple ceremony at the local country church. It was a picturesque, nineteenth-century English-style church where Rose and Marion sometimes prayed, although they never missed the vicar's traditional, old-fashioned services at Easter and midnight on Christmas Eve.

'Good heavens, Baz,' Daniel joked. 'Why don't you go for broke and hire St. Patrick's Cathedral?'

'Great idea — wish I'd thought of it myself. Can see the headlines now: *High profile businessman marries popular soap queen.* It's rather short notice, though; they're booked up months ahead, if not years. But maybe I can pull a few strings, might still be possible if you're willing to postpone?'

'Barry, I was pulling your leg. And of course we're not going to postpone. I've been waiting for this lady quite long enough. In any case, we've already talked to the local vicar and can't disappoint him. We'll have to do the best we can with the local church.'

'Let's hope for a fine day, then. We'll get someone to fix up stadium seating in the churchyard and relay the service outside through speakers.'

'The speakers, maybe. Seats in the churchyard, no. The poor old vicar would have a fit. He's never seen more than half a dozen in the congregation even at Christmas time,' Daniel muttered, beginning to think it might be simpler to ask Foxie to elope.

But Barry's mind was still running on expansion. 'That marquee you hired for the open day. Maybe we can get hold of it again. Have a really big do.'

'Barry, you're not hearing me. This is our wedding you're talking about and we don't want it turned into a media circus. Foxie's had quite enough of being the centre of attention. She doesn't want a big do.'

'She certainly doesn't.' Foxie had come into the kitchen just in time to hear what Daniel was saying. 'Bad enough that my mother insists on traditional white.'

In the end, she was able to convince Barry that the day would be less stressful for everyone if the guest list remained small.

'What else can I do for you, then?' He looked crestfallen. 'A trip to London maybe? A honeymoon in Noumea?'

'No thank you, Barry,' Daniel said firmly. 'We appreciate the thought but I have our honeymoon arrangements well under control.'

'I still think it's a shame,' Barry said, as Daniel ushered him towards the door. 'You're passing up the best excuse for a knees-up we've had for some time.'

'Then why not get married yourself, Barry?' Foxie gave him a quick kiss on the cheek. 'You can hire the Rod Laver Arena and have as big a party as you like.'

'No thanks.' He gave a shiver of mock distaste. 'I've got two demanding ex-wives to keep already. Three would be asking for trouble.'

★ ★ ★

Although Foxie was willing to humour her mother's wish and get married in white, she didn't want a conventional, modern wedding-dress. She went around all the vintage clothing stores but none of them had exactly what she was looking for, not even her special little shop in Royal Arcade. The others had dresses from the fifties with yards of fabric, finishing mid-calf and making her look like a Christmas tree fairy or a meringue on stilts. Brocade and glitter didn't fit the bill either. What she was really looking for was a well-cut dress from the thirties in satin-backed pure silk but even if such dresses still existed, treasured and wrapped up in tissue in camphor wood chests, they would be seventy years old now and probably too fragile to be worn.

She tried diaphanous hippie dresses from the seventies and even a sixties dress with flowing, medieval sleeves but nothing was exactly right. She returned home, tired and dispirited without having seen what she wanted at all.

Home again, shoes kicked off under the kitchen table and, with a mug of tea clasped in her hands, she reported her fruitless journey to Rose and Marion.

'I think I may have the answer,' Rose said. 'My mother was a seamstress years ago and like all good dressmakers, she could never resist buying quality fabric when she saw it at a bargain price. I still have a suitcase full of her old silks and satins that I meant to give to the Salvation Army, but somehow I never got round to it.'

'Rose, you're an angel.' Foxie gave her a hug. 'Let me see.'

It proved to be a treasure trove of more than just fabrics. There were braids and trims, cards of lovely antique glass buttons and a pale green enamel art nouveau clasp in the shape of a dragonfly. And there, at the bottom of the case, beneath lengths of red silk velvet and floral crêpe de Chine, lay exactly what Foxie was looking for — a bolt of satin-backed silk, the colour of rich cream.

'Take as much as you like.' Rose smiled at the girl who was almost too overcome to speak. 'Have the whole trunk as a wedding present.'

'Oh Rose, I couldn't,' Foxie protested. 'These materials are so valuable. You have no idea.'

'Those old things?' Rose wrinkled her nose. 'Not to me. I saw far too much of them when I was growing up. My mother had half-finished dressed hanging all over the house. If you don't want them, I'll only give them away.'

'Oh, I do want them. I do.' Foxie gathered the fabrics to her bosom possessively before Rose changed her mind.

After that, she had to spend some time running to earth a dressmaker of the old school, who knew how to manage delicate fabric cut on the cross and also to hand-finish a garment in the painstaking, old-fashioned way. She discovered a Russian lady who actually did live upstairs in an attic and used an old-fashioned treadle sewing machine. She came with extravagant credentials, allegedly from various crowned heads of Europe, so her services didn't come cheap. But, although her English was far from good, she accepted Foxie's sketches and pictures with enthusiasm and seemed to know exactly what she wanted.

And when the bride-to-be tried on the finished result together with a small coronet of waxed orange blossoms, also from Rose's treasure trove, she was delighted. Her wedding-dress surpassed anything she could have imagined. She hugged the little dress-maker, almost lifting her off her feet as the old lady nodded, beaming from ear to ear, taking pride in her handiwork.

Foxie looked as if she had walked right out of an early black-and-white movie; a cinema goddess from the thirties come to life. The fabric fell softly from the neck, cleverly cut to outline and emphasize her tall figure, making her as regal as a princess. There was even a short, manageable train to be caught up by a loop on her little finger, allowing her to dance. The sleeves were long and flowing, caught into a narrow band at the wrist and fastened with many tiny pearl buttons. On a belt just below her waist sat the dragonfly clasp, her only adornment. She had decided not to carry a sheaf of flowers but just a trailing posy of miniature ivy, white rosebuds and her favourite gardenias.

★ ★ ★

On the day of their wedding, Daniel arrived at the church, surprised to find himself the victim of a serious attack of nerves. The man of business, who could talk so eloquently and present a plan to a room full of people without a qualm, felt a fluttering in his stomach as if it were filled with butterflies. If he were to open his mouth just a fraction, he knew they would escape and fly around in the church.

Barry Glenn, who had insisted on standing up for him as best man, was no help either, continually turning around and reporting on the people he recognized, arriving to fill up the tiny church.

'The press, represented by Clare Mallis no less, sitting well to the fore,' he murmured, making Daniel wince. 'Good job I remembered to hire security. Don't want her gate-crashing the reception.'

'At this stage, Barry, I don't care what she does. She's the least of my worries,' Daniel snapped back. 'You do have the ring?'

'For the third time of asking, yes.' Barry grinned. 'I've been through this several times before, you know.'

'Once will be quite enough for me,' Daniel growled.

'Relax. You're getting married to the delectable Foxie. This is your lucky day.'

The only person who seemed to be more nervous than Daniel was the elderly vicar, surprised to see the pews in his tiny church rapidly filling with people. For the umpteenth time he checked the appropriate service and as the stout lady organist struck up a fumbled version of 'Here comes the bride' to announce Foxie's arrival, he looked up to see the girl he remembered as a leggy child walking slowly towards him on the arm of Harvey Watson — a radiant bride. The vicar sighed. The old-fashioned dress struck a chord in his memory, reminding him of the day he married his Sarah and how the sight of her had taken his breath away; until now he had never seen such a beautiful bride.

Harvey, spruced for the occasion and looking rather like Mr Pickwick, seemed proud as Punch to be asked to give her away. His wife was sitting with Rose and Marion in the front pew. Apart from a certain sparkle in her eyes, Rose seemed relatively composed while Marion, encouraged by sniffles from Mrs Watson, gave in to her emotions and sobbed uncontrollably, trying to stem the flow of her tears with an inadequate lace handkerchief.

Foxie's only bridesmaid, Laura, followed a

few steps behind, wearing a simple but flattering silk dress the colour of wisteria. She carried no flowers herself, determined to place herself in position to catch Foxie's bouquet. Marriage was on her mind. Having come to Australia on a temporary visa, she was determined somehow to stay.

'Cor, take a look at the bridesmaid,' Barry muttered to Daniel. 'Makes me think it *might* be worth getting married again.' He gave Laura what he hoped was his most charismatic smile and received a cheeky grin in return. She knew who he was.

'Hands off,' Daniel whispered back. 'That's my cousin and she's too young for you anyway.'

'Oops!' Barry said, rolling his eyes.

As the last strains of the organ died away, the vicar cleared his throat to address his unusually large congregation in sonorous tones.

' 'I am the resurrection and the life,' saith the Lord. 'He that believeth in me, though he were dead, yet shall he live'.'

'Ahem.' Harvey Watson was quick to interrupt. 'You're in the wrong service, Vicar.'

'So sorry,' the old man whispered, mortified. 'I do so many more of those.' With shaking hands, he hunted through his book, looking for the right place, giving a brief smile when he found it.

'Dearly beloved, we are gathered here in the sight of God and the face of this congregation, to join this man and this woman in Holy Matrimony.'

Intuitively, Foxie sensed Daniel's nervousness and smiled radiantly to reassure him. Everything about her was radiant today, he thought; her skin was luminous and even the fabric of her wedding-dress seemed to be glowing. Like a dew before morning sun, his nerves evaporated and the vicar, too, seemed to be gaining in confidence, his voice strengthening as he reached a dramatic point in the service.

'If any man can show any just cause why these two may not lawfully be joined together, let him now speak or else hereafter and forever hold his peace!'

'I can!' a female voice called from the back of the church, shrill with hysteria. 'That woman is already married — to someone in America! She has three children, as well.'

Daniel and Foxie looked at each other and groaned, recognizing Stella Patterson's strident tones.

'Oh dear.' The vicar took a step backwards, looking over his spectacles at the woman who was marching purposefully towards him. 'I hope you're quite sure about this?'

'Positive. She likes to call herself Marlowe now but her real name is Carole Parker. She's been married four times already. I don't know how she has the hide to stand up again dressed in white.'

'Now, Stella!' Her husband came hurrying up, trying to take her by the arm. As usual, she shook him off. 'Please don't do this. You're making a fool of yourself again.'

'Mr Patterson.' Daniel fixed him with a stern look. 'The last time this happened, you promised to get her some help.'

'I know. But she seemed so much better. I thought she'd got over it, especially when she said she wanted to see you married. I thought it was going to be all right.'

'Mr Morgan,' the vicar addressed them hesitantly. 'Jane. Are we going ahead with the ceremony or not? Bigamy is a serious matter and I wouldn't like to be a party to anything — '

'Vicar, I promise you. I am not and never have been married to anyone else,' Foxie said. 'This is the first time.'

At a click of the fingers from Barry, two security men appeared from the back of the church to take charge of escorting Stella outside, her husband trotting after them, shaking his head. Although the woman was still scowling, thankfully for once she remained silent.

'I'll have words with them, after,' Barry muttered to Daniel, giving the security guards a meaningful look. 'They should never have let her in.'

Clare Mallis, hot on the trail of what she hoped would be a good story, slid out of her seat and hurried to catch up with the Pattersons.

Fortunately, the rest of the ceremony went without a hitch and the wedding guests, including the vicar, still apologizing for his gaffe, met up again at a local hotel where a private reception had been arranged.

Although Barry Glenn made an elegant speech to Daniel and his bride before dinner was served, his good taste didn't extend to their send-off. Daniel discovered his car trailing yards of white toilet paper and rattling tin cans. Big red heart balloons were tied to the radio aerial and *Just Married* was scrawled in white paint across the back window.

Having said their farewells at the hotel, they put up with the noise of the clattering cans as they drove down the main street. But as soon as they left the revellers behind they stopped at a service station to remove all the evidence and clean up the car. Before doing so, Daniel switched off the engine and turned to Foxie.

'Mrs Morgan,' he said slowly, testing the words. 'I think I'm going to like saying that. I might even get used to it. Have I told you that I love you, Mrs Morgan?'

'Not in the last five minutes.' Foxie leaned towards him to receive his kiss. 'I love you, too.'

'Oi!' Someone leaned out of a car behind them. 'Get goin,' you two! You'll have time enough for all that on the 'oneymoon.'

'Talking of which, where are we going for the honeymoon?' Foxie asked.

'It's a surprise.'

'You told me to bring my passport, so it has to be overseas.'

'I'm not to be drawn.'

'I shall find out anyway, soon as we get to the airport. We're going to New Zealand again, aren't we?

'Maybe.' A smile twitched Daniel's lips.

'Oh, yes. Don't you remember? You know how I loved the Bay of Islands and promised to take me back to spend more time there. And, knowing you, there's probably a horse or two you're thinking of buying. Shame not to make good use of the trip while we're on the spot, even if it does mean mixing business with pleasure.'

307

'You know me too well, Foxie.' He sighed, shaking his head. 'I'm never going to surprise you, am I?'

'I don't need surprises. I've had quite enough of storm and tempest already. I'd like to think of our marriage sailing upon seas calm as a millpond.'

He gave a bark of delighted laughter. 'Not very likely, is it? Given your volatile temperament.'

'Oh? Now look who's talking,' she started to say.

'Oi!' The voice from the car behind intruded again. 'Are you lovebirds gonna move or do I have to come and push your car out of the way?'

★ ★ ★

The hotel Daniel had chosen was one of the most luxurious at the top of the town and their room had panoramic views across Melbourne. A bottle of French champagne had been left with the compliments of the management, together with a plate of handmade chocolates, and the room was fragrant with white gardenias as big as camellias. Daniel had remembered her favourite flowers.

Although Foxie had been unable to find a

wedding-dress at her favourite vintage stores, the shop in Chapel Street had provided a beautiful black silk and lace nightgown with a matching peignoir. Although it was from the 1930s and still in the original box, it had never been worn. She changed into it while Daniel was taking a shower — she suspected he really wanted to shave — and she sat in front of the dressing table, brushing her hair.

He came out, wearing a black silk dressing-gown and smelling of something she now identified as Aramis. She had bought an extra bottle for him as part of his wedding present — just as he had given her a bottle of her new favourite, Silver Rain. He had also bought her a beautiful antique Victorian gold locket on a chain.

'Snap!' he said, recognizing they'd both chosen black before sliding an arm round her waist and leaning down to kiss her. 'This fabric is almost as delicious as you are,' he murmured when they came up for air and swung her into his arms, ready to take her to bed.

'It seems a shame to unwrap such a lovely parcel but I think we should,' he said as he dropped her in the middle of the king-sized bed and let his own dressing gown fall to the floor. 'I wouldn't like to tear the wrapping.'

Taking a very long time about it, they made

love without protection for the very first time. There was no haste, no urgency now; they had the whole of their lives ahead of them and the future was looking good.

Sated, Foxie lay back on the pillows watching Daniel open the champagne with a minimum of fuss and pour the pale gold liquid into two crystal flutes. He passed one glass to her, toasting her with his own.

'Here's to you, Mrs Morgan,' he said. 'And may your loveliness be passed on for generations yet to come in the large family we're going to have.'

'A family!' she said, clapping her hands to her face in mock horror, melodramatic as Carole Parker at her best. 'Oh Daniel, what have we done?'

'What is it now, Foxie?' He sat up on one elbow to stare at her, half believing she was serious. 'What's wrong?'

'Our children! They'll all be red-heads. It's a very strong gene.'

'So?' He gave his characteristic shrug. 'It didn't do us any harm.'

'No? What if they have violent tempers as well?'

Daniel lay back on his pillows and laughed. 'It's too late to worry about that now. You should have thought of all this before we got married.'

'You railroaded me. You didn't give me time to think about anything.'

'Oh, so now *I'm* to blame?' His eyes began to sparkle dangerously. 'I never knew such a woman for making an argument out of nothing.'

'It's not nothing!' Highly emotional after making love and almost provoking a quarrel, Foxie grabbed her peignoir and shot out of bed to go to the bathroom.

What was the matter with her? It was the happiness; it was all too much. She didn't know if she wanted to sulk or to burst into tears. Perhaps she was pregnant already? That would explain it. Thinking maybe a warm bath would soothe her and calm her nerves, she bent to turn on the taps.

Daniel heard the small shriek that told him she wasn't alone in there. He smiled inwardly, waiting for the summons that came only moments later when she peered at him anxiously around the bathroom door.

'Would you believe it?' she said. 'In a first-class hotel like this. There's a spider in the bath . . . '

We do hope that you have enjoyed reading this large print book.

Did you know that all of our titles are available for purchase?

We publish a wide range of high quality large print books including:
Romances, Mysteries, Classics
General Fiction
Non Fiction and Westerns

Special interest titles available in large print are:
The Little Oxford Dictionary
Music Book
Song Book
Hymn Book
Service Book

Also available from us courtesy of Oxford University Press:
Young Readers' Dictionary
(large print edition)
Young Readers' Thesaurus
(large print edition)

For further information or a free brochure, please contact us at:
Ulverscroft Large Print Books Ltd.,
The Green, Bradgate Road, Anstey,
Leicester, LE7 7FU, England.
Tel: (00 44) 0116 236 4325
Fax: (00 44) 0116 234 0205

Other titles published by
The House of Ulverscroft:

FLYING COLOURS

Heather Graves

With a broken romance behind her and a promising future ahead Corey O'Brien intends to concentrate on her chosen career. She certainly doesn't expect to come to the attention of someone like Mario Antonello, a racehorse owner and heir to a fashion house . . . Their first meeting isn't friendly so she is surprised by the interest he shows in her later. It all seems too much and it will take a while for Corey to find out the truth. Then she discovers a shocking secret and feels she must turn her back on him forever.

EMILY'S WEDDING

Patricia Fawcett

With her wedding date fixed and her mother powering ahead with the preparations, Emily puts aside her niggling doubts about Simon and his refusal to talk about his past. Corinne is making the wedding dress, but she is a woman with problems of her own, not least her troubled relationship with her son Daniel, who hides a terrible secret . . . It is Emily in whom he eventually confides as the two find themselves drawn inexorably together. Pulled in all directions, she is faced with a dilemma — and her wedding day is fast approaching . . .